About the author

Fred Turner is an author born and living in Stockport. He lovingly describes the town as a collection of people and buildings. He graduated with a degree in History in 2012, commenting that the experience of learning about past injustices gave him a unique and historical perspective into his own uselessness. Since then he has worked in a variety of charities in Greater Manchester, supporting people with their mental health, people who are homeless and migrants in the area.

It is the injustice sanctioned by the state that gives Fred his desire to write. He explains that his fiction is an outlet to draw attention to the misery created by authorities and power holders. His stories are inspired by the voiceless experience of people oppressed, ignored and powerless.

Soldiers

Frederick Turner

Published by Armley Press, 2023
ISBN 978-1-9160165-7-6

Copy editing: John Lake
Cover art: Agnieszka Januszkiewicz
Cover design: Mick Lake
Typesetting: Ian Dobson
Production: Mick McCann

Acknowledgement

Thank you to everyone who has taken the time to read and to listen to me going on about this book and to everyone who has shown support and patience.

Soldiers

Chapter One

Hearing the curator of the local history museum talk, you would think that the whole of human civilisation had pivoted on the successes of Milltown. He pounced on those who entered his dusty and underfunded museum, lecturing them about the town. He explained it had been central to the Industrial Revolution, played a key role in the Civil War, been a key conquest by the Romans, and was probably the birthplace of culture. Past inhabitants had won back the Holy Land in the Crusades and had been heroes in the Battle of Britain, at least according to one piece of research he once read. He would swell with pride as he proved Milltown's historical importance.

The truth was a little less grand. Milltown was on the periphery of a much larger, older and historically significant town. Outside the imagination of the curator, Milltown was brazen in its insignificance. Prior to the Industrial Revolution, it had been a small collection of villages. The inhabitants had slaved to provide agricultural produce to the larger nearby town. With the dawn of industry, this changed. The river allowed for the construction of cotton mills, and poor people flocked in from the countryside to sell their labour to the factories offering work. Coal mines to the north fuelled this industry. The goods were then transported to the larger town and sold. As more was produced, more people sought work in the squalor, and so the working town grew. Industry developed and the town lurched from boom to bust. All the while, the suffering of the poor remained constant.

Into the twentieth century, slowly the mills closed. Cheaper non-unionised labour was found among businesses abroad. Other industries came and went, but by the 1990s Milltown was not able to sustain its population in work. The wealthier workers travelled to other towns to work; many left for good. The rest sank with the town. Work disappeared and so did aspiration. Dire social policies of the 1980s hammered the town and its population, stamping out any trace of respect that labour brought. Who can feel self-respect if they have no activity to make themselves feel respectable? While other regions of the country grew richer, bleak forgotten towns like Milltown shrank into even darker corners of history. The unemployed had no prospect of escape. They were no longer needed to labour; they felt like they were no longer needed.

It is a shame that the old curator, rattling around the local history museum, was so infatuated by populist history. Because there was a real history to tell here. A history of exploitation and oppression. A history of labouring people who had worked to the bone for centuries. Working people who, when they sought higher wages, had their jobs stripped away from them. Working people, no longer working, who would send their children to school to learn skills. Finally, children in school, waiting to leave and, if their spirits were not crushed, who fought their classmates for the few jobs that remained. Centuries of labour had resulted in nothing for the people who had worked. Only misery.

A local park offered a view over the town. Positioned on a hilltop, it looked over the valley where the town centre was built. Standing above the town, you would see the red brick structures of the converted and decaying mills still there. The skyline was littered with high-rise tower blocks. In need of renovation, their visible decay was a reminder of current social policy. Looking over the town you would notice rows of terraces towards the centre. Of course, from this standpoint you would also see the shining and tireless lights of supermarkets; what town is not lit up by the intrusive advertising of consumerist havens? Looking down the valley, on a clear day, you would notice the houses change. The tower blocks and rows of terraces ended. There was much more space and many more trees. In that direction, the more prosperous neighbourhoods stood, away from the cluttered centre.

Milltown, redundant, at the end of its labouring history, tired and exhausted. The concrete structures of the town were almost sighing with the effort of existing. The local buses rolled around town in a disinterested manner. The central shopping centre had less atmosphere than the local crematorium. The town was bleak.

*

This was the town that Abdul’s family was about to move to. This Friday the family had taken their last trip to the mosque. With prayer finished, they were gathered just outside the doorway. Abdul's mother, Awet, spoke with two women who had heard of their impending move. Interested in other people's affairs, they had ambushed Awet. Abdul's father, Tarek, was a short distance away, also speaking to some acquaintances. Ibrahim, Abdul's older brother, had gone off with some friends, while Abdul remained with his mother.

A few weeks earlier, Abdul would have been playing with Ibrahim. He had never been shy, and enjoyed socialising. He and Ibrahim would often be together. But recently, he had hardly been detached from Awet, his mother. As the family waited to move, it was hard for the others to picture Awet without her youngest child somewhere about her, leaning against her leg or even clinging to her skirt. It looked odd for a seven year old boy, but he didn't want to leave her. Awet accepted this. Sometimes she felt a little embarrassed to have a son clinging to her and wondered what people may think of him. On the whole though, she was sympathetic. In many ways, his clutching to her expressed a feeling she felt inside: not wanting to leave, wanting closeness.

'So we heard you're leaving, Awet. We'll be sorry not to have you around any more,' stated one woman.

'You'll be missed. But we hear you've done well. Your own business,' stated the other.

'I suppose you have to take these opportunities when they arrive. How often do you get chances like this?' presumed the first.

Awet interjected, lest the conversation *with* her became a conversation *about* her: 'It was a hard decision. We spent a lot of time thinking about it. We'll not be too far, though, and will come back often.'

'Of course, decisions like that I suppose you need to mull over,' said the first.

'How have the children taken it? A big step for them.'

The first lady replied. 'It will be scary at first, of course, but they're quite resilient, really, as soon as they get settled.'

Awet again pushed her way into the conversation. 'I think it has been a bit of a shock but to be honest they have taken it OK...'

'That is good news,' said the first lady, glancing at Abdul. 'You know, my sister moved from Sheffield to London because of her husband's work. It took ages to find a school place though...'

'Ah, I remember this...' said the second lady.

Awet gave in. She stood quietly, accepting the conversation about her did not require her input. Smiling politely she withdrew to her thoughts, absent-mindedly stroking Abdul's hair. Between well-timed nods, she went over their preparations. Was everything packed? What would they need to purchase? She considered ideas for decorating the flat, whether she should buy new curtains. All of this depended on how much she would have to spend. Her husband had assured her that there were no issues with money. She still made contingency plans.

Her thoughts moved to tomorrow. She was inviting friends over for their last weekend. She still needed to prepare some food and make sure the house was clean.

Her thoughts moved to her son. Her husband Tarek had hardly noticed the change in his character. She, on the other hand, was constantly reminded of his misery. From an outgoing young boy he had quickly become sullen and introverted. She worried about him. He had been so settled, never expecting to be dragged away from his friends and extended family. Sometimes she cried for him at night. She continued to stroke his hair softly. All she could do was hope that, when the time came, and he began his new school, he would settle quickly.

She smiled as the two women rattled on. In the background she heard the sound of her husband's voice.

A few feet away, Tarek was repeating what had become a monologue. Wherever he found a new audience, he launched into a presentation about his new life and business. He articulated with humility the unexpected chance that fate had thrown him. Working quietly had not gone unnoticed and finally he had received a reward for his patience. His uncle had left him a shop in his will. Ostensibly humble, he said that he was not going to waste this chance; he was going to take the bull by the horns and not let this opportunity escape him.

'He was ever so clever, my uncle. Always seeing opportunities to progress his business. He had a businessman's brain. A real example to us all, really. So this shop in Milltown, if he had been with us longer, I know he had plans. He saw the gap in the town, the space to expand. I have been looking at the local area. There is such an opportunity to expand there. Lots of empty commercial space you see, and the rents are very cheap...'

The other two men were watching him talk. They had long since given up trying to interject. They nodded when appropriate, but Tarek needed no encouragement.

'So I have planned, you see, I have done the finances. By living above the shop, we are maximising the financial position. It may be a bit cramped for the short term, but that way we will save more quickly. We will have, say 12 months, 24 maximum, before we can look at more properties. As long as the market stays favourable, I expect we can invest quickly...'

In recent weeks he had become a self-certified expert in the local economy of Milltown. Had he acknowledged that he was speaking to an accountant and economist, he may have been a little more modest.

Awet tired quickly. The chatter of the women before her and the relentless drone of her partner made her feel uneasy. She made excuses and turned to her husband. The women, still talking, hardly acknowledged her departure.

It took Tarek a second to notice his wife and son standing next to him.

'Tarek...'

'So the shop, from the documents I have, is large enough to put an extra aisle through the centre...'

'Tarek...' she repeated.

'Oh, dear, I was just telling them about the new shop we own...'

'I know, I'm very sorry, but Abdul is very hungry, as is Ibrahim. He has not eaten since lunch. The girls will be home now too. So I think we should really go.'

'Of course, of course...'

Before Tarek could start again, one of the men seized the opportunity.

'I think we must also be going, my wife will be waiting with food as well...'

Wishing Tarek the best of luck and hoping to see him soon, they left. Unabashed, Tarek smiled at Awet.

Calling Ibrahim, the four of them returned to the car. Tarek walked slightly ahead, his head high. Awet, solemn. This would be the last time she was here for some months. She felt saddened thinking of friends she would be leaving. Abdul also felt this sadness as he walked closely by her. Ibrahim, a little older than Abdul, appeared not to notice their graveness. Of all the family, he was most enamoured by the image his father had painted of the exciting future awaiting them.

In the car, Abdul sat quietly looking out of the window. He talked little that evening.

Chapter Two

A homelessness assessment officer in Milltown Council opened a letter. She read the notes, sighed and turned to her colleague.

'I told Mr. C that he needed to get information from his doctor if he wanted to be rehoused,' she said. 'So, he's got his doctors to say he has depression. Didn't look depressed when I saw him.'

'Not changing the decision, then?'

'Nope,' she said. There was a noticeable smirk on her face.

Her name was Silvia. Her role was to assess homeless people, or those at risk of homelessness, to check whether the council had any duty to rehouse them. She dictated whether a person would have shelter, and exercised this power mercilessly. There was no room for emotive arguments in this functionary's mind. She would seek hard facts, interrogating the poor, ensuring that no-one received a service they were not definitely entitled to. Being too harsh was better than being too lenient and letting the 'piss-takers' scrounge off the council. She was a pious crusader defending the council's resources like the Holy Land, against the mendacious scum that came like leeches to feed. (It is a shame that the actual Crusades were not fought over a few run-down council flats in a backward town, as it is unlikely Saladin would have wasted so much life in winning them back.)

Devastated people returning to sleeping outside had often compared her to a Nazi. Her appearance may not have looked out of place at an SS ceremony. Her dyed blonde hair was pulled back against her scalp so severely that the creases on her forehead were no longer visible. She wore a contemptuous look. She could use subtle facial expressions to show disbelief and disdain. Her suit, masculine in style, highlighted the social gulf she perceived between herself and the downtrodden. If Edward the first earned the name the

Hammer of the Scots, Silvia could justifiably be labelled the Taser of the Poor.

She placed the letter on a neat pile of similar material on the desk. She started her reply, thanking Mr C. for the new evidence, but indicating that many people needing homes had depression. Being rehoused, she wrote, was not essential to his condition being alleviated, and that his doctor would offer more appropriate support.

The office was windowless and, when full, very cramped. As it happened, most of Silvia's colleagues were not at work, with it being the first week after Christmas.

A customer service assistant came to the door. Standing awkwardly, he waited to be acknowledged. Silvia eventually looked up.

'Yes?' she asked.

'Yes, er, there's a family here. They say they're homeless. They're just in reception.'

Silvia sighed.

'That's fine. I'll be down shortly.'

The assistant mentioned he would put them in an interview room and shuffled away.

'No rest for the wicked, eh, Silvia?' said her colleague.

'None. I'll keep them waiting for a moment. Would you like a drink?'

After making a drink and chatting some more with her colleague, Silvia descended to the office. As she marched towards the interview room her persona changed. Her lips pursed and her walk became slower and more deliberate. She straightened, rigid, almost visibly freezing over.

The interview room was small and unaccommodating. It embodied the confrontational nature of Silvia's work. Two doors gave access to the room, one for the customer and the other for staff. The room was separated by a wooden desk that formed a barrier across the entire room.

Inside the room sat a blonde, pale woman. Her roots were showing and she had huge bags under her eyes. She was hunched over, looking at the floor. As Silvia entered she sat up. At the woman's feet, a young dark-haired boy was playing with a toy car. The boy also looked pale. One small suitcase lay against the wall. The lady smiled meekly, not quite sure what to do.

Silvia placed herself down. She had perfected a routine: slowly and deliberately she would cast her eyes over the family; she would not speak until she had laid her paperwork on the table and filled in the date. If a person had the audacity to talk to her, she would not answer back until she was quite ready.

If the victims were not so desperate, they would have found this melodramatic routine laughable.

Silvia looked up, straight into the other woman's eyes.

'Do you want to tell me your name, sweet?'

Her tone was cold.

'Jane Crosby, and this is Darren Blackwater.' Jane said. Tiredness, stress, anxiety led to her being completely overwhelmed. She was in shock from her experiences the previous night.

'Hmm.' The silence resumed as Silvia filled in the sections on the sheet. 'But you are his mother?' she said after a moment.

'Yes' replied Jane.

She took the basic details of the family. Their last address, their citizenship, their dates of birth and address history. Then she resumed her focus on Jane.

'So. Let me clarify. You are homeless?'

'Yes.'

'You can't live with your parents any more?'

'No.'

'Have you lived in Milltown before?'

'No.'

'But you are from the UK?'

'Yes'

Silvia was repeating questions. She felt like a detective interrogating a potential criminal, getting them to slip up.

Meanwhile it crossed Jane's mind that the interrogator had early onset dementia.

'You were living with your parents recently?'

'Yes.'

'And you left because....' This was the first point in the interview that Silvia invited Jane to elaborate. Jane was taken aback. She took a second to answer. Silvia raised her eyebrows slightly.

'Because last night the house was attacked...'

'The house was attacked?' Silvia asked. Her tone remained flat.

'Yeah, attacked.'

'And who would attack your parents' house, sweet? And do you have evidence?'

'Well the police came, you can call them.'

'I will do, we have to investigate everything forensically. I suppose you don't have a crime reference?'

'No, it all happened...'

'Too quickly,' Silvia answered for her. 'I think we are most interested, now, in who would attack the house.'

The way Silvia inflected her tone maddened Jane. Her tiredness evaporated and she now felt irritated. Who was this woman asking these questions? She had come here for help.

'I already told the police last night. I think it was linked to my ex-partner. He was...'

'Abusive, I'm guessing.'

Jane frowned. Interrupted again. She had a burst of adrenaline and asked, 'Why do you need to know this? I don't have nowhere to sleep tonight. With my son.'

Darren responded to her more assertive tone. He looked up at her.

Silvia had been waiting for this. She laid her pen down on the desk and looked straight at her. Most interviews peaked at this point: the interviewee stepping out of line, questioning her authority in her interview room. She spoke:

'It's relevant, sweet, because I have to check that we can help you legally. So I need to know every detail. I have to decide if you are actually homeless, and I have to know if you are intentionally homeless. Then I can say if we can help.'

She sat back quietly looking at her.

Jane made a last jab: 'So, what, you gonna leave a mother and child on the street? We don't have anywhere to go.'

'We would never leave a child on the street.'

Silvia was flexible with the truth. Even if the mother was found to be intentionally homeless, she was entitled to support legally, for a limited time.

Silvia smiled at her, waited a moment, then began again.

'So you had an abusive partner. Was this the boy's father?'

'Yes.'

'How long were you together?'

'Until August last year. Seven years maybe.'

'Hmm.' Silvia made some notes and looked at what she had written. Then she looked up again.

'So. You left him because of the abuse? Then you went to your parents, and then here.'

'Yeah.'

'How did you get away from this abusive man?'

'He was really aggressive one night, and the police showed up. They took him and I ran away.' She was answering as curtly as possible. She felt humiliated.

'Why was he so aggressive on this night?'

'Something about money, I think.'

'Hmm.' Silvia wrote more notes.

'Did you engage with any support agencies about the abuse?'

'Yes.'

'The police took him from the maisonette. What I'm wondering is why you didn't stay there? If he was gone, surely it was safe?'

'It was his flat. I was too scared to stay there. Me and Darren had seen a lot there.'

'It sounds like it. However, it was a place to live. I'm inferring that it was safe, as he was not there, and secure. Maybe you left too quickly.'

Jane's stomach turned at this point. Just the thought of staying there caused her anxiety. 'It didn't feel right staying there. I didn't feel right there.'

'Do you have any mental health problems?'

'What?'

'Mental health. Depression, anxiety?'

'Yes... I have pills from the doctor. It's been a really hard few months, especially for him.' She indicated towards Darren, who had settled down to play again.

'Well, we may need some medical evidence to say you couldn't stay there. You were at your parents' for four or five months?'

'About that, yeah.'

'And you left because of the attack, but you don't know who it was?'

'Well, who else could it be?' she answered, her tone edging towards sarcasm. Silvia took one of her characteristic pauses.

'The police attended?'

'Yes.'

'Do you not think that maybe, with the police, it may have been safe to stay there? I mean, it does not seem like there is any tangible evidence of who did this attack. Is there?'

'I just wanted to keep my parents safe. I didn't want to leave. We loved it there, but I was making it dangerous for them.'

'What did they say?'

'Nothing, I left before they could stop me,' said Jane, her eyes filling with tears. She had not wanted to leave, and had wept, writing a letter for her mother.

'So you came here, to Milltown, even though you have never lived here. You have no local connection here; your son has no school here?'

Jane picked up on Silvia's implications. They were sharp, cutting into her.

'I know it may not seem clever, but I wanted somewhere I could make a fresh start. Where I wouldn't be known. And it's a bus journey to my parents' house.'

'It's a long bus journey, sweet.'

'I know...' Jane was mid-sentence and Silvia rose. She said she would be back shortly and needed to make some checks.

'What's gonna happen?' asked Jane as Silvia was leaving.

'Wait here, I need to make some enquiries.' She left Jane in the empty room. Jane felt a sense of relief.

Silvia returned to the office where her colleague was making a drink.

'So, how did it go?' asked her colleague, half-listening as she poured hot water into the mug.

'Usual sob story,' said Silvia. 'No local connection, and sounds like they could have stayed where they were. Probably intentionally homeless, but I can't prove that today.'

'Oh dear,' said her colleague. She returned to her desk and noticed a Post-it note she had scrawled on.

'The Crawler family didn't show up for the flat,' she said.

'What? After all the whinging?' said a frustrated Silvia, looking up from her loading computer screen. 'They will be intentional, now, as well. I'll ring social services in a second to update them. Did they call themselves? Did they give a reason?'

'Yeah, two. First, too far from the kids' school....'

'They're homeless,' stated Silvia, 'they should take where they're given. Move school if need be.'

'And they heard the area was rough. They weren't impressed from the start that it was a hard-to-let. Anna was fuming. They need to fill that flat today, and no one will take it. They can't lose another week's rent on it.'

Silvia shook her head irritably. Her computer loaded up and she looked at an e-mail.

'It's on the hard-to-let list, so we can put anyone forward for it.'

'Hmm,' said Silvia, now only half engaged.

'I can't get through to anyone on my list, but what about that family in the interview room?'

'Hmm... what? No. She can't just rock up here and be given a flat.'

She was outraged; this equated to rewarding recklessness.

'I know. I know. But, I got their details from reception and I already did an informal police check. I also spoke to their last landlord. No issues except the domestic violence. They could sign today, and it would buy us a bit of favour with Anna.'

'There's absolutely no one else?'

'It's a hard-to-let. Even if we speak to anyone, they all know the block and no one wants to live there.'

Silvia sighed. Pragmatic realities often interrupted her ideological crusade.

'Fine, then. I'm going to make a few more calls, just double check a couple of these details, then I'll speak to them.'

Two hours later Silvia returned to the interview room. Still in the room Jane, fed-up, was encouraging an irritable Darren to play. They looked up as Silvia wandered in.

'Do you have any details of your income? Unemployment benefit? And the child benefits?'

Jane rummaged in her bag and found the paperwork. Silvia glanced over them and said, in a despondent manner:

'This is all in order. A taxi will collect you shortly and take you to the housing office. A flat has become available.'

'What?' said Jane, shocked.

'Yes. A flat has become available. You need to sign today. If you don't take it, you will be intentionally homeless and there will be limited help for you.'

'Of course, we'll take it.'

Jane breathed in deep. Her low spirits were overtaken by the adrenaline of relief. 'Thank you so much.'

'Hmm,' said Silvia. 'You need to make this tenancy work.'

She left the room.

The taxi came, took them to another office and they signed for a flat. Due to the rush, they were not given the chance to view the property beforehand, but were assured it had been brought to a lettable standard.

They arrived at the property. It was a second floor flat in a small four floor block. There was a poorly maintained communal garden, and graffiti decorated most of the walls. The block was on a backstreet and faced a second block on the dead-end street, making it feel cut off from the surrounding terraces. The property was unfurnished, meaning Jane had to apply to a local assistance scheme for beds and other furniture and appliances. There was always a delay between signing for the property and receiving the goods.

That night, in a flat lit by the street light shining through the curtain-less window, having eaten a cheap takeaway, listening to the music of another tenant through the wall, the mother and child slept on a cold floor. They had managed to buy three new duvets in lieu of a bed, so lay on one and under two. It was bleak. Jane, lying awake watching over her boy, was overwhelmed by worry. She hoped her parents were all right, she hoped she had removed herself far enough away from danger. She hoped she would be able to make this empty structure a home.

Chapter Three

One winter morning, a week after the Christmas break, Abdul sat in his classroom in Milltown. He wore his red uniform, which, when bought first-hand, was bright red. This was an unfortunate choice of colour: a family's wealth could be seen in how faded the child's uniform was. If you were to line up the twenty-nine children in the class, with the most faded jumper at the back and the brightest jumper at the front, the line would be in order of richest to poorest. Abdul would be at the faded end. His father had suggested that Awet buy a second-hand uniform to save money.

Abdul was looking out of the window. He had finished the maths exercises already and the boy next to him was copying his answers. He was not discreet as the teacher was disinterested. She was leaning against the door-frame, chatting in a hushed voice to a colleague. Thoughtlessly, they didn't realise that by whispering the young ears in the class listened all the harder. They managed to hear that the other teacher, who had the headteacher's son in her class, had made him stand at the front of the class all morning. She appeared quite delighted by this. His misdemeanour had been minor and the teacher knew that the punishment was harsh, but she had a gripe with her employer. So the son got punished.

The weather was grim and threatened rain. As morning break approached, the teachers worried that they may be stuck inside with the children without a chance to get their coffee.

As break arrived, they bundled their classes into the playground and rushed towards the staff room.

The staff room displayed a whole array of teachers; every type we witnessed in our journey through the school system. They queued to get their coffees (one had herbal tea). At the front of the queue was the young, new, enthusiastic teacher, yet to have their optimism trashed; waiting at the back was an older teacher, a disillusioned veteran of the education system. This old teacher had seen too many young minds appear inspired, only to watch lives shatter their aspirations. After forty years of service he carried in his heart an overwhelming sense of pointlessness. At a desk sat the deputy headteacher, with a coffee made for them. They had an unbearable passion for marketing the school. The deputy head could get so enthusiastic about this below average school that the old veteran felt that, should the deputy's career go down the pan, North Korea would employ them in their state media. Next to the deputy was a newly recruited teacher who had trained later in life. They perhaps had the most balanced outlook, keeping focus on the main reason for being there: it paid the mortgage.

Abdul's teacher was in a transition period. She was young enough to remember wanting to help young minds, but had seen many losing interest at high school. She sat in the corner nursing a coffee. Next to her sat the wet weekend teacher of the school. She was the type who got a bit tearful at weekends, when she felt that the children in her class didn't really like her as a person. She was the type who dreaded the parents' evening, being overwhelmed by having to explain herself to disappointed and judgemental parents. She sipped her herbal tea.

The wet weekend blew her nose and turned meekly to Abdul's teacher.

'I meant to ask,' she said in her nasal voice, 'how has that new boy settled in, the Muslim one?'

If the wet weekend had been more perceptive, she would have noticed Abdul's teacher raising her eyes to the ceiling. She was not in the mood for this conversation again.

'He seems much better than he was. You remember I was saying he was quiet. Always on his own. A few weeks before Christmas he got in with Brett's group. Seemed a bit more cheerful. Was nice to see him actually playing with other kids.'

The veteran teacher, sitting nearby, was listening out for a conversation where he could play the grumpy sod. He snorted at this.

The wet weekend said, 'Must be hard being one of the only Muslims in the school. Especially in this area.'

'Hmm,' said Abdul's teacher.

'Brett...' said the veteran, shaking his head. 'There's a kid that will go far in the wrong direction.'

Abdul's teacher nodded. She knew exactly what he meant. The wet weekend blew her nose again and carried on looking miserable.

The grumpy veteran continued, 'I hate swearing about the kids, I really do,' (he had called every child in the school every swear word he knew at one point or another) 'but that one, Brett, is a knobhead. No two ways about it. Bully, talking back, careless about work. Not surprising, considering the parents... Arrogant. Most arrogant I've met. Spent parents' evening last year assessing me... Abdul is better off a loner than with that knob...' Abdul's teacher settled down for the lecture. She planned her evening meal in her head.

The wet weekend looked really down in the dumps. She pulled out her handkerchief and blew her nose again; she hoped that Brett would not end up in her class next year.

As the teachers took their caffeine fix, in the cold playground the children were playing.

Abdul had, since starting school, been seeking acceptance in the large group of boys from his class. He had slowly been accepted in this group and, by the end of the last term, had played with the other children. This had been nice for the teachers to see. He had slowly begun to feel a warmth of social acceptance. It was not like his last school, but he was feeling better.

This break time, Abdul behaved how he had done at the end of last term. Not bold enough to raise his voice in the group, he stood near them, hoping to be included.

The group of about twelve boys from the class acted roughly the same each break. They would gravitate towards Brett and his two closest cronies, as if waiting for orders. Brett's size and confidence gave him a level of sway over the group; he had no qualms throwing his weight around. His hair shaved to his scalp gave him a fierce look.

Brett had a more privileged background than those around him. Most of his peers were poor, while his family had a secure financial position. They acted with snobbery. Brett's father was the regional manager of a chain of pawn shops. His role was to ensure the shop workers acted with the necessary viciousness, while maintaining a friendly and caring service. Perhaps desperate customers were comforted by smiling shop assistants while they were being ripped off.

Brett's father had a darker side. He was a local activist for an essentially racist party. The party, horrified at Britain being less white than they thought it used to be, met in a local pub. Brett's father relished rallying local people against foreigners who had 'come over here and taken their jobs'. The party never discussed global inequalities that caused jobs to evaporate, only a conspiracy of foreigners seeking to inconvenience local folk. Brett's father never mentioned that his own company employed foreign people as you could pay them less than the minimum wage with no complaints. The politically forgotten people of Milltown were starting to accept this party; no mainstream politician offered them any alternative understanding of their poverty.

Brett's father was a man who revelled in asserting his limited power over others. Brett was already displaying similarly vile characteristics in the playground. This week, the father had noticed the Muslim boy in the school.

As the children gathered round Brett, he informed them of his desire to play chase. He selected someone to be 'it' and everyone got ready to run off. Just before they did, Brett raised his hand for attention.

'Wait!' he shouted. The group stopped.

He turned to Abdul. He pointed at him maliciously.

'You can't play.'

'Why?' asked Abdul meekly. His brown eyes opened wide.

'Because you're a Paki. Get lost!'

Brett shoved him. Not so hard as to make him fall, but enough that he faltered backwards.

The children all ran off. None thought anything of it. Abdul didn't know what he had just been called, nor, until this point, had he felt any different to the other children. Now he felt different. Like he didn't belong. Dejectedly, Abdul wandered away to another part of the playground. His shoulders slumped and his head dropped down. A tear came to his eye but he didn't want to cry. He didn't want to be noticed. Surrounded by children playing in the noisy school, he was alone.

Brett's actions led to the other children in his class treating him like he had the plague. He spent the next few days cast out of the small society in which he lived every day.

Eventually, wandering slowly through the playground on his own, he came across two boys in the year above him. They were playing quietly just behind a wall. One had large glasses and a patch over his eye. The other was tall with bright ginger hair. The shorter boy with the patch, who had been acting as a pirate, noticed Abdul watching them.

'Hi,' he said. 'Who are you playing with?'

Abdul didn't want to answer. He shrugged his shoulders.

'You wanna play with us?'

The boy had an innocent charm. He was over-friendly. The taller boy, more reserved, smiled.

'OK,' said Abdul. A seed of optimism grew again. Perhaps he wasn't a complete social pariah. The boys became friends fast.

Unaware of the racial term Brett had used towards him, not knowing what a 'Paki' was, Abdul wondered whether this ginger boy and his spectacled friend were Pakis as well.

Despite no longer being alone at break times, the unfortunate truth was that Abdul had little to look forward to at school: lonely diligence in the classroom and a sad hope that these new friends would be around during break. At home, things were not much better. His parents worked nonstop and he spent less time with his brother. Abdul was getting used to his own company.

*

His mother never stopped worrying about him. Despite working tirelessly in the shop with Tarek, she noticed her younger son's sombreness. She tried to speak to him at times, to find out how she could help. It was hard to get answers out of him.

One evening as she closed the shop she turned to Tarek, sitting at the counter.

'Tarek, can we talk about Abdul?' she asked.

'Hm, yes.'

'Have you noticed him lately? He is so quiet. He comes home from school and sits in his room. I ask him about friends at school and he looks like he will cry. He has changed so much.'

'Hm,' replied Tarek. He was a little distracted counting the day's takings.

'I just don't know what to do with him... Tarek?'

Realising that this conversation wouldn't just go away, Tarek looked up and acknowledged his wife. He did his best to look sympathetic.

'We knew things would change, coming here, and it may be hard. It has only been a few months and he still needs to settle.'

Awet replied, 'I know, but he doesn't seem to be getting better, Tarek...'

'Listen, Awet, I know it's hard to see him change, but maybe this is a good thing. A challenge for him early on. He will learn to deal with problems like a man. When my father came to this country he had nothing, he knew no one, and he succeeded. Perhaps people need to go through hard times to come out stronger. He will be strong. Just like Ibrahim. Ibrahim is doing OK.'

Awet faltered. For whatever reason, Ibrahim had really done well on their move. He had lots of friends and often stayed out so long he missed the evening meals.

'Trust, Awet! Everything will turn out well.'

With this, he came round the counter and kissed his wife on the cheek. Awet went upstairs to the flat.

*

In their small flat, Jane sat Darren in front of the television. She had bought it second-hand today and was quite pleased. It had taken some time and a lot of frustration to get it tuned but Darren was enjoying a programme now.

She went to the kitchen to get some tea. Opening the box of tea bags, she saw she had only one left. Having no money to do a shop until next week, she put the box back. She took a cup of water from the sink.

Her phone began to ring. It was her mother.

Dawn, Jane's mother, had been calling two or three times a day. Usually there was little to say, but Jane was happy for the calls.

'Did you get the TV working, Jane?'

'I did, Mum. It works fine.'

'Your dad would have come over, you know, he said he would.'

'I know, but it's over an hour on the bus and I got it sorted. Don't worry.'

'OK. And you're sure you’re OK for money? I can bring some down if you need it. We get the pension tomorrow.'

'Mum, don't worry, we're getting things together. A local charity have been really helpful. We got some furniture and everything. We’re doing OK. You've given us enough over the past few months.'

'We just want to make sure you're all right, Jane. You can always call if you change your mind and we'll be right there.'

Jane accepted this.

'We'll have to come and see the flat soon, too, and I miss my little Darren, how is he?'

'I'd love you to come, but maybe when it's in better shape. Darren is OK. I'm really surprised. I thought he would be really affected by it all, but he just seems to be himself... after everything I've put him through...'

Jane had to stop talking to hold back a tear.

'Eh, Jane, listen, you haven't put him through anything. It was that father of his. You're both safe now. Away from it all.'

'I know...'

There was a moment's silence on the phone.

'Listen, Mum, I need to check on him and then get him to bed. I'll speak to you tomorrow.'

'OK, look after yourself.'

'Say hi to Dad for me.'

'I will... goodnight.'

The phone call ended and Jane returned to Darren. He was falling asleep on the floor in front of the television. She picked him up and carried him into the bedroom. They were still waiting for his bed to be delivered from social services, but a charity had given her a mattress for the time being.

With Darren in bed, Jane returned to the main room of the flat. She looked around for a moment and then sat in front of the TV on a dining chair until she felt herself falling asleep. She had little energy. The past few days had been so busy, running from place to place. She had hardly remembered to eat.

As she moved to the bedroom she went over everything she had done, from sorting furniture for the flat to getting Darren enrolled in school. Milltown was all unfamiliar. Finding offices, shops and other places was difficult and she had no one to ask.

Now and again, she had noticed herself jumping when she saw people who looked like her ex. She was constantly looking out for him, wary of danger. She knew she needed to be calm, for Darren's sake as well as hers.

She lay down on a pile of duvets. She thought about what she needed to do tomorrow. She also thought about the times she had been with her parents. She missed them.

Chapter Four

Abdul and Darren were both shaped by the forgotten Milltown. This town, historically industrious, presently redundant, could chronicle in its bleak history the nurture of these two boys into men.

Abdul grew up in the small flat above the shop. He spent most of his primary school life either alone or in the company of his two friends. At home, his parents were often distracted. His father worked tirelessly and Awet worked long hours with him. Tarek didn't want to hire employees if they could do the work. This left Abdul in the care of his siblings. His older sisters soon left for university and, due to the cramped conditions of the flat, were rarely inclined to return. By the time Abdul was eleven, his brother watched over him through the quiet weekends and evenings. In lieu of a friendship network and family life, Abdul focused on his school work and reading. He became used to his own company.

As he reached high school he was a loner. His two friends, the tall ginger boy and the spectacled shorter boy, had gone to different schools, leaving Abdul friendless. He had learnt to go unnoticed, so rarely received attention from classmates. In class he kept a low profile. Marked by bad experiences at primary school he couldn't face being directly ostracised by his class. Self-imposed exile seemed more dignified. He did get the odd comment, sometimes racist, but was never bullied like some of the other boys in the school.

In his school work, he had excelled. His parents encouraged him to take school seriously and he had no other activity to occupy his time.

He enjoyed being taken to his extended family, but as he grew he felt an emotional distance there as well. The tireless work of his parents meant that these trips happened rarely.

The constant in his life was his mother. She was always concerned. Although she worked hard and didn't spend so much time with him, they still had a close bond. She worried about him and encouraged him when she could. Inside, she felt a guilt about Abdul that she didn't feel for her other children, as if she had let him down.

Now in his sixteenth year, having excelled in his exams and waiting to start college, Abdul was spending the summer working in his father's shop. Tarek was finally in a position where he was looking for premises to open a second shop, and was often absent. This had left Abdul and his mother working together for much of the summer.

Late in the summer, as Abdul waited to start college, Milltown was hit by a heatwave. The mud in the park dried to dust and much of the grass became yellow and brown. Walking in the streets, Abdul found himself thankful for even the slightest breeze. The strongest indicators of the heat however were the men and women of the town, whose clothes became more and more revealing. Abdul, walking through Milltown, would find himself fascinated by the topless men with beer bellies dropping over their shorts. A thin boy himself, he couldn't imagine what it felt like to carry that much weight. He was even more concerned by the young women. Tight and revealing clothes displayed large parts of their breasts and denim shorts revealed the curves of their arse cheeks. Looking, staring, at these women, he was sure he could sometimes even see a nipple on their poorly covered chests. Abdul's reaction to this was multi-faceted. A virgin, he was aroused by this and couldn't help looking at the women. When he saw them sexual thoughts entered his head, images based on the porn he had sometimes watched online.

Part of him was more judgmental. Their dress was so different to the women he saw at the mosque. He felt so different to these people walking around revealing themselves; he found them vulgar and sexually intimidating. Perhaps because he was conservative, or just because he didn't feel part of this culture, part of him looked down on people flaunting themselves so publicly. He knew he would never know how to talk to people dressed that way. He had

had little experience with women and had rarely spoken to them.

Today, Sunday, Abdul had walked through the park on his way to his brother's flat. He was particularly perturbed as, lying in the park, there had been a young but very muscular topless man. As he walked past, Abdul had observed him. While not the most muscular man he had ever seen, something about him drew his attention. He had sandy blond hair and a young-looking face. Abdul had taken in every detail. In fact, despite trying to repress it, he had been sexually attracted to this man. He had never felt like this before and he began to worry. The person aroused him but it was a man! He had mentally castigated himself for these thoughts and doubled his pace towards his brother's flat. He could run from the park but couldn't run from his biology, and it was a battle to suppress these feelings. As he walked, the sexual images involving this man kept coming into his head. They would get to the point where he was imagining both of them naked on a bed, making out, before he stopped his mind going any further. He also worried that in these thoughts he was so passive in this man's arms. Why was he imagining being dominated?

He reached his brother's flat. About half an hour's walk from the shop, the flat was in a converted semi-detached house. There was a one-bed ground floor flat and the small one bedroomed flat upstairs in which Ibrahim lived. It was a pleasant area. There were trees on the street, it was near the park and there was a small garden at the back of the house. The garden was terribly overgrown. The grass was knee high and brambles covered the edge of the garden. A young child would imagine tigers and lions hiding in the long grass. Neither Ibrahim nor the ground floor tenant felt that garden maintenance was their responsibility. Unfortunately, neither did the landlord; he had the advantage of not living in the property, so cared very little about maintaining the garden.

Having been buzzed into the flat, Abdul ascended the stairs and entered. The door was already open. He walked through the small landing and into the dark living room. The curtains were not yet opened. The dark made the room feel cave-like. There were clothes everywhere and takeaway wrappers covered the floor. Abdul opened the curtain to look onto the overgrown garden. While the light made the room feel less murky, it highlighted the squalor. He made some space on the small coffee table, moving a pair of boxers and jeans, and placed down the bags he was carrying. He noticed the television was on.

He then went through into the kitchen. It was smoky, and Abdul saw that the fire alarm had been disconnected. The sink was filled with plates and there was food left out on the surfaces. He was happy that his brother was eating, and still using plates, but wished the flat was kept in better condition. He opened the small window.

He heard Ibrahim rattling around in the bedroom at the front of the house. He coughed. The type of cough which lasts a while, where there is still something disturbing the throat and chest that the coughing person can't quite clear. Eventually he shouted through, 'I won't be long. Get yourself a drink.' Abdul knew he would not be able to find a clean cup.

Abdul found the kettle in the lounge and brought it back to the kitchen. He found damp instant coffee, with its lid open, in the fridge, but no milk. He decided to begin cleaning a little while he waited. As he cleaned, he disturbed the fruit flies that had been resting on the kitchen surfaces. He made space, returning food to the fridge and cupboards, wiped down the surfaces and began washing the plates. He was going to dry the pots as well, but when he found the dish cloth his stomach turned. It stank. He thought back to his biology lessons and visualised the bacteria crawling over it. He flung it into the washing machine. He made a mental note to bring washing powder next time. The kitchen looked marginally better and he was happy with himself.

Ibrahim entered the living room and threw himself on a sofa. Abdul went through. He passed him a glass of water and looked at his brother. He was pale and tired. There were large bags under his eyes and his hair was unwashed. He was sitting in jogging bottoms but no top, displaying his growing gut. Every act seemed laborious for him. Abdul watched as he strenuously rubbed his eyes or scratched his shoulder. The light and heat were bothering him.

Even around family, Abdul was quiet. He didn't have the character to start conversation and would happily wait silently for the other person to interact.

He watched his brother. He cared for him and felt awful seeing him in such undignified conditions.

'I'm sorry little bro, I'll be with it in a minute. I was working last night.' Ibrahim's voice was still croaky from sleep.

This was the pattern when Abdul visited. He would spend time waiting for his brother to wake up; when his brother eventually became more talkative it was usually time for Abdul to leave.

Ibrahim yawned.

'Are you working tonight?'

'Yeah, seven nights in a row now,' replied Ibrahim.

'He should hire more people.'

'Tell me about it.' Ibrahim shook his head. He leaned over to an ashtray and looked to see if there was any cigarette left still worth smoking.

Ibrahim was working nights in a takeaway. Like Abdul, as a teenager he had spent hours working in the shop. Unlike Abdul, he had made a closer group of friends at high school. For reasons that a psychologist, a sociologist or even an astrologer may explain, Ibrahim had been better at socialising. There had grown a contradiction between his father wanting Ibrahim to provide cheap labour at the weekends and Ibrahim wanting to spend time with friends. This culminated in Ibrahim moving in with a friend at seventeen, and eventually into his own place. He had worked at the same takeaway for some years now and it was draining the life from him. He was like a plant growing in a dark corner that the sun never reached. Wilting and fading, he looked too exhausted to even try to seek the sun any longer.

Unsurprisingly, his enthusiasm for cannabis had developed into a habit and then a habitual dependency. He often reassured Abdul he could stop whenever he wanted. And he could. Then he would start again a few hours later.

Abdul broke the silence by indicating the bag he had left on the coffee table.

'Mum sent you some dinner.'

'Thanks, Abdul. I miss her cooking.'

'You should come round more, Ibrahim. She misses you...'

'I know, I know.'

Their father was rarely a subject of conversation. Ibrahim and Tarek would often argue. This hurt Awet. The two had been close when Ibrahim was small. Over the years in Milltown, she had watched her family splinter.

Ibrahim coughed again. Abdul didn't want to ask his next question but felt compelled. In the pause between Ibrahim coughing and Abdul speaking, the insipid Sunday morning television show could be heard.

'You still smoking, Ibrahim?'

'Less and less Abdul. I know it's bad.'

'It is.'

In part to change the subject, in part because he meant it, Ibrahim said, 'Mum told me about your exam results, Abdul. You're a smart kid, you know.'

Abdul smiled.

'I mean it Abdul, you won't end up like me, keep learning, and studying and everything, and you just remember me when you're a doctor or lawyer.'

'I will,' Abdul smiled, his first smile of the day. 'You can still do more, you know. You were smart too.'

Abdul had really looked up to his brother when he was younger, but their roles had become inverted. As he had grown older, Ibrahim had started to spend more time with friends, leaving Abdul on his own. Abdul didn't resent this.

He knew the stress that Ibrahim had been under from their father. Now he felt like he needed to support his brother, but really didn't know how. He watched Ibrahim stuck, struggling with the rent and spending money on weed. He felt like his brother was just treading water; he worried that he would slip under with barely a ripple to show where his life had been.

Abdul was about to encourage Ibrahim to come to the mosque with the family next week.

Then, the buzzer went.

Ibrahim, sloth-like, got up. As he moved he made noises like a man double his age; grunts punctuated his every action. He muttered into the telecom by the door and buzzed the newcomer into the flat. They heard heavy footsteps on the stairs and the front door opened. Before the newcomer entered the living room he shouted through:

'Hey, Ib, the brother in Windsor Tower is dealing again, so I picked up some strong shit.'

He finished his sentence as he entered the living room, a huge bag of weed in his hand. The stubbly, young and peaky face of Ibrahim's friend looked embarrassed as he noticed Abdul. Ibrahim looked similarly embarrassed. Abdul was known in Ibrahim's circle of friends, and they considered him a bit stuck up.

The newcomer got his good humour back. He looked at Abdul briefly and then at Ibrahim saying, 'There's enough for the three...' He smirked.

Abdul was a mix of embarrassed and disappointed. Doing nothing to improve the image of a stuck-up younger brother, he stated, 'I'm just going.' He made his way to the door.

Behind him as he left the room he heard his brother and friend laughing. He was halfway down the stairs before Ibrahim caught him.

'Hey, Abdul, I'm sorry about him,' he said. He looked genuinely sorry.

'It's OK. I'll see you soon, hopefully.' The two brothers smiled at each.

Abdul set off home. Ibrahim got stoned.

Chapter Five

On this hot summer afternoon the thirteen-year-old Darren sat with a group of friends in the concrete communal garden between the two blocks of flats. Oxford House and Cambridge House faced each other in an almost intimidating manner across this concrete court, which was decorated with dried and wilted flowers. The group was about twelve strong, three of whom Darren was close with; the rest ranged from eleven to seventeen, hailing from the surrounding estates.

This was an eclectic group. Boys and girls, younger and older, all assembling in the same space. They were left to their own devices: some had parents forced to work anti-social hours; others had parents who just didn't have the energy to be with their children for long periods of time. Darren was in the latter category. They were left to play out and entertain themselves.

They got a bad press.

One old lady was particularly unimpressed with the teenagers assembled on the court. She would peer out of her ground floor flat window and watch them. Mrs Shallowfax, the widow, was sure these children were up to no good. She waited, ready to call the police at the slightest misdemeanour. She believed that the children were a sign of the end of civilisation as she knew it. The kids were out of control, loitering, hanging around, being anti-social, doing nothing constructive, wasting away. Although she had not seen them being intimidating, she knew that they might be. When she left the flat, she would do so only when they were not there and hoped to return without having to walk past them. When a housing officer called in on her, she would labour their ears about the need for national service; the children needed discipline.

You may debate the merits of placing guns in children's hands and training them to kill. Mrs Shallowfax didn't think this far ahead. She just wanted the alien mass moving away from the entrance to her block. The poor widowed lady, ageing and in poor health, paranoid about a group of children. She had many empty hours in her days, just like the young ones that she feared.

Darren saw different people come and go in the group. On the whole, there was very little criminal behaviour, despite the accusations of Mrs Shallowfax. Twice, Darren had witnessed a member of the group spraying a wall. In one instance it had actually been quite funny, as the young girl with the can had no idea how to use it. Instead of writing that one of the people in her school was a 'wanker,' she managed the first three letters only. The letters were so smudged you wouldn't even realise she had been using English. As she attempted the fourth letter the police had arrived, and Darren remembered the adrenaline of running from them. He ran faster than he had ever run.

A few of the people in the group also enjoyed shoplifting. This was another adrenaline kick that Darren loved. There was something really enjoyable about heading into a shop in a group and dodging the security. Darren only enjoyed this in the supermarkets. When they targeted a local corner shop he was overcome with guilt. He remembered his mother speaking with the shopkeeper when he was young and really did not like the feeling of stealing from him. The faceless supermarket with the security guard was a much better rush.

Today, Mrs Shallowfax was spending a day with her sister, who lived over an hour away. While Darren was hanging around the block, she was boring her sister with observations of how life was not the way it used to be. Her feeling was that humans were degenerating back into apes.

Had Mrs Shallowfax been watching the young people, she would have seen a new and malicious character standing among them. A young female had attached herself to the group. She was a young shabby haired girl, a lot more active than the rest in the group. When she laughed, her whole body bent over with an exaggerated cackle. Her arms moved wildly and her whole body language was intimidating. Her clothes were dirty and mismatched to the point where you might think it was purposeful. Her black short-sleeved top contrasted drastically with her orange shorts. Her trainers were red.

Darren, sitting on the bench, had been quiet today. He was aware of this new character and was unsure where she had appeared from. He noticed her vocal behaviour and was encapsulated by it. When she talked, she addressed herself to the whole group; when she moved or joked she ensured all eyes were on her. She spoke without waiting for answers, and when she asked questions they always sounded like demands.

Darren couldn't estimate her age, though he guessed about fifteen or sixteen, especially as she wore bold makeup and spoke very sexually. She didn't seem close to anyone.

Today the group had been very inactive. The warm weather was not conducive to movement. The new girl was exhibiting her boredom through mindless acts. She had been kicking the bench behind Darren for a couple of minutes. Prior to that, she had been jumping on the dry earth in a concrete flower bed. Suddenly she jumped in front of everyone and pulled out her cigarettes and a lighter. She tried to light the cigarette but the lighter failed.

'Fuck this!' she exclaimed. She threw the lighter on the floor. 'Fucking dodgy stuff from the Paki shop.'

She looked around. She noticed everyone was watching her.

'Who else smokes?'

One of the older lads in the group passed her his lighter. Again, it didn't work and she threw it on the ground, this time more forcefully.

'This is a fucking joke.'

At this moment Darren noticed an Asian boy walking quickly past one of the blocks. Darren had seen him cutting through the estate on a number of occasions. He recognised the boy from school. He didn't know his name and always felt a twinge of pity for him. He was in an older year group to Darren.

The new girl also noticed this boy. Her eyes under the dark eyeshadow lit up. A smirk crossed her face.

'That's him from the shop,' she said. With no word to anyone she skipped over to him. He continued walking fast. Some in the group followed her.

'Hey, hey,' she yelled as he passed. He stopped and looked up. 'What's your name?' she asked innocently.

'Abdul,' he answered. He did not look straight at her. She had now positioned herself right in front of him, so he couldn't get past. Swept up in the movement, Darren moved closer.

'You got a lighter, Abdul?'

His whole body language screamed he would rather be anywhere but there at that moment. The contrast of the young girl and Asian boy was something to behold. She stood, intimidating and he cowered, aware of the size of her group of associates.

'I don't smoke,' he said. He added, 'Sorry.'

He began to move away, but she still stood in front of him, a nasty smile across her face.

'You sold me a shit lighter, can I have a new one?'

'Sorry,' he said, making a move to go, but she still blocked his path.

'I need a lighter... why don't you smoke?' she asked.

Abdul didn't know what to say. He stood still.

'I need to go,' he said.

'Why don't you smoke? Does Allah not let you smoke? I never saw a Paki smoking before.'

She cackled at her humour. Abdul saw his time and scurried past her. She followed him closely, berating him with questions about Asian people smoking, about Muslim rules on smoking. He ignored her, hoping desperately she would get bored if he just kept walking.

She flipped from comic to angry.

'Hey, don't ignore me, you ignorant fuck,' she said. Her face was strained as she got angry. With all the force she had, she pushed Abdul hard. He fell to the floor and she stood over him. This amused her, and she was struck with another bout of her cackling.

Darren looked at the young Abdul on the floor. He noticed his dark, wide eyes staring up at her, almost pleading. Darren felt his insides turn. He didn't find this funny. In fact, it upset him, watching him frightened and intimidated when he had done nothing, absolutely nothing, to deserve it. He could imagine how the poor boy felt. Deep in his mind he was driven by a memory of his mother at the mercy of his father.

'Hey,' he said. 'Leave it.'

'He sold me a bad lighter, so he's gonna give me a new one.'

'Leave it,' said Darren more forcefully. 'He doesn't fucking have one.' He stepped forward and noticed he was taller than her. He straightened himself up and made it clear he was not asking but telling her.

She spat on the floor next to Abdul and walked off.

'Someone gonna get me a lighter...' she said walking off. She did not walk in a straight line. She stamped her feet as the whole crowd returned to their original spot. Abdul had already gone.

For the rest of the afternoon there was a frostiness among the group. The new girl kept making digs at Darren. Darren was annoyed, but quietly absorbed her blows.

*

Late that evening Darren returned to the flat in Cambridge House. Looking about, he noticed the door to his mother's room was still closed, as it had been when he had left. He knew she had been out as there was some money on the side next to an unopened packet of anti-depressants. He called through to her to see if she had eaten.

'Can you get yourself some tea, Darren?'

He was used to this. When her anxiety was high she would spend days in bed. She always saw to his needs one way or another. He bought some food from a local convenience store, and spent the night watching TV.

Since moving to Milltown, Jane had struggled. She had done her best for Darren, but all her attempts to improve things had gone awry. She had failed to get jobs and had become more and more anxious. She became worried in crowds and was haunted by her past. She had no support in the area, no friends and no family. They would visit her parents sometimes, but not as often as she wanted to, being worried she may be noticed in the town. She was desperate not to put her family in harm's way.

She had gone to the doctor about the depression and anxiety; he had given her stronger tablets. They just made her sleepy and she hated them. She rarely took them unless she was feeling really low. She had learnt to try and just ride out the low feelings, waiting for her mind to become more positive again. The moods would come, like a mist descending into a valley. She waited for them to clear.

As Darren had grown, he had learnt to do things himself. He would do the cooking, and even started to do some cleaning. From a young age he had taken himself to school. School was always difficult. He didn't like lessons and often found himself in the bottom sets. He had learnt in class that if he just sat there long enough without saying a word the teacher would just give him the answers to the questions. He did enjoy sports class, though.

It was hard with a mother whose moods made her so reclusive. He knew she would come around eventually, that they would have a good few weeks where she would be attentive before drifting back into another depression.

When his mother was depressed, he liked to sleep on the sofa. The living room was closer to the main door of the flat, so he felt that if something were to happen, he would hear it first and call for help.

As he lay on the sofa he kept thinking about the Asian boy lying defenceless on the floor. He felt awful. The image upset him. His grandmother had taught him empathy, and his first thought was always the way others may feel. He hated seeing people bullied.

As his eyes were closing, an advert for the army came onto the screen. He had never paid attention to these before, but this evening the images of the heroic soldiers resonated with him.

Chapter Six

A few mornings later, Darren was surprised to be woken by noise from the kitchen. He had fallen asleep in front of the television again, and could hear movement. He entered the narrow kitchen and found Jane on her knees with her head in a cupboard, rooting for something.

'Mum...' he said.

She looked up to see him in the doorway and smiled at him. She told him that she wanted to make him breakfast, but couldn't find the cereal. There was none, he had been eating toast for breakfast. Jane smiled and put some bread in the toaster. She put the kettle on as well to make them both a drink.

'You're feeling better, then, today?'

'Yeah, a bit. Still tired, but feel like I can get about a bit.'

She looked at Darren, still standing in the doorway. She took him all in. She couldn't believe how quickly he was growing. In high school now, tall, with his dark hair, and athletic. She was proud of him. He had been through more than most people his age, with the violent father, the moves and now coping with her in her depressions. But he managed. He never showed any resentment.

The years had worn Jane down. She was a shadow of the woman who had once defended Darren from his father. She looked at Darren through tired eyes. The bags under her eyes reflected the strain showing in her face. She had become thinner with age. She had stopped dyeing her hair; her natural brown was now littered with grey. Her most noticeable characteristic was her nervous disposition. Perhaps it was her slightly lowered head, or uncomfortable stance, but something told any onlooker that she was not happy in her skin. If the earth had opened to swallow her up, her last emotion would have been gratitude.

Jane ushered Darren back into the main room and the two of them sat on the sofa together. The TV was on quietly in the background but neither took any notice.

Darren had eaten half of his toast and turned to Jane, who was sitting quietly, considering life. She was perched on the edge of her seat.

'Thanks for breakfast, Mum,' he said.

'It's no problem, Darren. You do so much round here, it's the least I can do.'

She smiled at him.

As he finished his toast a thought occurred to him. If he could get her out of the house, it may be good for her. She had not been out for over a week. He looked at her and said, 'We could go to Nan's today. I've not been for a week.'

Jane didn't acknowledge him at first, then turned to him.

'I suppose... well, we could... but I was going to do the washing. It's nice out.'

Not getting a firm no, Darren tried again.

'It will be sunny tomorrow. I know they want to see you.'

'Hmm,' replied Jane. Her mind had wandered and she went quiet. The thought of leaving the house had triggered her anxiety. This was always lurking beneath the surface of her consciousness, ready to creep out.

She said she didn't feel up to it, and said that he could go.

'When you do go out, can you buy some washing powder? I think I have some money for you.'

From the pocket of her dressing gown she produced a ten pound note and gave it to Darren. He said that he would.

She looked at him again then looked away.

'I don't think I'm up to going out yet, but give me a few days,' she said.

Darren nodded. They both turned to the TV.

Jane had become quiet. When she was emerging from a depression, there were always false starts. It seemed to Darren that she was pushing herself to get better. He knew that she was trying for him, and he appreciated it.

He was bothered that she was going out less. Especially as she was not seeing her parents and they kept asking after her. They were finding it harder to get to Milltown as their walking was getting worse. It was hard for him to understand why she didn't go there. For him, the bad memories seemed like the distant past. They had lived quietly since coming to Milltown and, really, not much had happened to them since arriving. For Jane, returning to her parents and the area in general induced panic. At every corner she worried about her ex-partner, or some associate of his, coming for her. She could find no peace there.

Darren got changed in his room then headed towards the door of the flat. He put his head into the living room before leaving. He noticed on the TV another advert for the army. He stood quietly watching it. It was short, but encouraged him to be his best. The idea of being paid to achieve physical perfection called to him.

Before turning to leave he said:

'You know, I may sign up for the army in a few years. What do you think?'

Jane was hardly listening. She was fixated on a thought from the past.

'Yep, a small box will do. Thanks again, Darren, I mean it,' she replied.

Darren left.

*

Abdul entered the small kitchen of the flat above the shop. He was cooking over the gas hob that evening. His parents were downstairs in the shop.

The flat had been very cramped when he was younger. He had shared a room with Ibrahim and the combined living room and dining room were often cluttered with people's belongings. Now it was just the three of them, the flat felt less suffocating. Ibrahim lived alone and his two older sisters had long since fled the family home. One had her own husband and family, the other pursued a career in nutrition.

Abdul stirred the spaghetti he was cooking. As he absent-mindedly spooned in some pesto, he thought about his week. Since visiting Ibrahim, he had not left the flat. He had stayed in on his computer and done bits of work in the shop. The assault, being pushed over in the street with the racial abuse, still hurt him. He kept getting flashbacks to the moment, lying on the floor, breathless, expecting to be beaten by the group of people. The thoughts made him nauseous.

There was no one he could speak to. His parents worked, his brother was getting stoned, and Abdul had no friends. He tried to suppress bad memories like this, forcing them back into darkened corners of his mind.

It was just one of many memories that lurked in the depths of his subconscious. Occasionally surfacing, they dragged him back to a miserable moment of fear or sadness or dejection. Every feeling he experienced, momentarily back in his head, a misery subverting his present. Within his mind there was a tapestry of sadness and miserable experiences: from the most recent assault to isolation in high school to his primary school and the bullying he received from Brett. He had spent a wealth of time being either physically or emotionally pushed to the margins of whichever human community he was trying to engage with. He would dwell on these moments. Then he would snap back, pushing the thoughts away. Sometimes he almost physically wrought himself out of the memory, repositioning himself in the present. It did not do to dwell on these things, he told himself. There was nothing he could do.

He shook his head. As he did so, he heard the door of the flat open and his mother enter.

'Abdul, are you here?' she called.

He replied he was.

She appeared in the kitchen.

'It is quiet downstairs so your father has sent me up.'

'There is enough for two if you want some...' Abdul indicated his spaghetti.

Awet looked at it. For a second she debated cooking her own food. She quickly changed her mind.

'You are a good boy, Abdul, looking after me.' She smiled and rubbed his arm. She took two plates from the cupboard and they sat down at the table in the main room.

With each year that had passed in Milltown, Awet appeared to have aged three. From a young-looking and happy woman, she had become worn and downtrodden. Her eyes were the most telling illustration of her tiredness. Where once they had been wide and bright, engaging and intense, they now seemed to look past wherever she held her gaze. The skin around the eyes was tired, making them appear to sink into her face. She was no longer a ray of sunlight able to brighten a room, but a wisp of cloud hardly noticed in a cloud-filled sky.

They ate quietly to start with. Abdul's thoughts were elsewhere.

'It was a quiet day,' said Awet. 'Your father is annoyed. It seems every time he gets close to saving what he needs he is pushed back a step.'

'He'll get there.'

Tarek had found a location to open a new shop. A loan had been agreed but the conditions of the loan were harsh. He was on the edge of gaining the capital he needed.

'Have you heard from Ibrahim today?'

'Not today.'

'Me neither. I hope he is OK,' said Awet. 'How did he look when you saw him? Was he still pale? He was so pale when I last saw him. He does not look after himself.'

'He was pale. And still smoking.'

Awet shook her head. She worried for Ibrahim and his unhealthy life, and she worried for Abdul and his quietness. With Abdul, she felt less worry. She felt, as he had done so well at school, he would succeed at college, go to university, and flee just as his sisters had done. She was sure that when he got to university, and was surrounded by scholarly types, he would be in his element. It was just getting him through. Ibrahim seemed a lost cause.

'I worry about him. He got into such a bad crowd. I am so glad the same did not happen to you. You always had more sense.'

Awet sighed.

A sigh can be expressive. It can say many things that a single word does not cover. Here, Awet, letting go of a small amount of air in her lungs, said much. Worry, exasperation and stress were all rolled into one with this sigh. Years of endless concern and feelings of getting nowhere with her older son were breathed into this small portion of air. Perhaps most poignantly, the sigh seemed to say, *if only we hadn't come here, things may have been different.*

'I spoke with your sister earlier. I told her about your exam results. She will send some money for you. I told her not to, but she was very happy for you.'

Abdul smiled. This was the first acknowledgement he had received from the family outside Milltown.

'I tried to get Tarek to agree for us to go out and celebrate, as well. Maybe with your sisters, if they can get here. But he is so focused at the moment, Abdul, I'm not sure he was listening.'

'It's OK. There does not need to be a fuss.'

'You did the best from all my children. A little fuss won't be a bad thing,' said Awet.

Abdul was touched by the thought.

'Did you write back to the college, did you decide what to study? You should call your sisters, they may have good advice, you know.'

'I may do. I think the sciences are the best ones. I did well in them and there are always jobs for scientists.'

Awet smiled. 'You can do any subject, Abdul. But your father, I think, wants you to do business studies. But maybe I will tell him the class was already full, what do you think?'

Abdul smiled and nodded. Out of everyone, she had always encouraged him, but also pushed him to make his own choices.

Abdul and Awet both finished their food. Abdul went to take her plate, but she batted his hand away.

'I'm still your mother and I don't need a carer yet,' she smiled, taking his plate. Abdul sat quietly, dwelling on college.

He was looking forward to college. It seemed like a fresh start, putting school behind him and getting a chance to really build on his knowledge.

He returned to his room and the computer. He heard Tarek arrive a little later but didn't go out to see him. He eventually went to sleep.

Chapter Seven

Unlike Darren, Abdul had a father for his whole upbringing. His father was distant, focused on his business and his sense of self-esteem. Emotionally, he neglected Abdul. However, there was no doubt in Abdul's mind that he was a good father. He worked and provided for the family. His children accepted that Tarek was working to ensure their wellbeing and create a business to hand over to them.

As Abdul was starting college, he felt distant from Tarek, but still looked up to him. He knew he worked hard and made life secure for him. Aside from bullying and general loneliness at school, he had been *all right* growing up. Abdul could even justify the way his brother had been treated. He understood that Tarek had only wanted Ibrahim to focus on the family business. Awet's views were similar. While missing her son, she didn't doubt Tarek's intention to provide for his family, however emotionally hurtful it may be.

A few months into his college career, Abdul was still living the same solitary life. He worked hard at college, worked hard in the shop, and visited his brother when he could. He had little time to himself, but little to do with spare time when he had it.

One evening, his father had requested he clean graffiti off the side wall of the shop. The shop with the family home above it stood on a main road in Milltown. It was part of a double semi-detached structure, with a small alley on one side and a takeaway selling fish and chips connected on the other. The area felt cramped due to the cluster of shops on the street and the tight rows of terraces behind.

For the past few months, on a semi-regular basis, the shop had been targeted by racist graffiti-makers. Three times, the family had woken up to find the side wall on the avenue sprayed with such catchy lines as 'Pakis out' or the equally disturbing 'White Power.' Tarek always insisted that Abdul clean the wall after nightfall, leaving the graffiti on the wall for the day. Embarrassed that they were cleaning it themselves, he would tell customers he was paying a company to remove the graffiti. He felt it added to an image of affluence. It unfortunately meant that the nasty statements were left on the wall the whole day for everyone to see.

While Abdul scrubbed the wall this cold clear evening, Tarek was inside going over his loan offer for a second shop. He was so close to establishing his empire and it was all he thought about. Awet was in the flat upstairs completing orders for the coming weeks. Having removed the spray paint the best he could, Abdul went inside. It was quiet. Tarek was reading behind the counter and there were no customers. It felt still.

Abdul carried the soapy water and bottle of strong chemicals into the storeroom at the back of the shop just behind the counter. In the poorly lit room, stacked with recent orders, there was a sink by the door. The door to the storeroom swung closed behind him.

His father was a few feet away, perched in the shop. The counter at the back of the shop had a view down the two aisles so Tarek could see the whole shop. Tarek was going grey now, and his face was much more wrinkled than it had been when they first moved to Milltown. He still maintained the same energy with customers, believing that the nicer he was the more likely they would return. He was like a coiled spring – quiet and still, then bouncing into action when a customer came through the door. Abdul really felt he missed the point of a local convenience shop; people would come regardless, due to the convenience and lack of other open shops. His father was convinced he could charm the whole neighbourhood into spending their money. He would refer to his uncle when citing this theory.

The bell for the shop rang as the shop door opened. Two tall men in thick coats entered. One carried a black bag loosely in his arm. The two men looked about themselves. The one with the bag approached the counter.

'Hello, gentlemen,' said Tarek, getting up. He placed extra emphasis on the word *hello.* 'How may I be of assistance?'

The two men acted strange, but Tarek had seen all sorts of people since working here. He was never perturbed by the public. The man approaching was pale and looked miserable.

'Cigarettes,' he grunted as he reached the counter.

'Of course, sir.' Tarek turned around to the packets behind him. 'Any brand in particular?'

The second man returned to the door.

Tarek was struck by the behaviour of these two men.

'Any brand in particular, sir?' he said again.

The man placed his black bag on the counter.

'All of them,' he said quietly. There was something alarming about this man's tone. He sounded both threatening and hurried. 'All the boxes in this bag, empty the till, and don't waste time.'

Tarek turned around slowly. Adrenaline was pumping through his veins. He started to shake, heart beating, mind racing. What to do? He watched in panic as the man slowly pulled a bat out of the bag and rested it on the counter. He noticed the man's gloved hand clutching the bat.

'You fucking deaf?' he said with quiet malice.

The second man stood impatiently at the door, watching through the window. Now and then he paced away from the door, returning seconds later.

Tarek was frozen. In the eight years of owning the shop, aside from some shoplifting and anti-social behaviour, there had never been something so serious. He did not know what to do. There was no way past this man.

The man with the bat had no time for this. He smashed the bat on the counter and yelled his demands again.

Now Abdul, in the store room, was aware of the situation just feet away from him. Like his father, fear gripped him and he was as immovable as a frozen corpse. He became aware of his deep breathing and tried to control it, lest the attackers outside realise he was there. He became aware of every slight noise his body made. Water filled his eyes.

'Empty the till, you Paki cunt!' came the next demand. The bat smacking the counter. He was losing his patience.

Abdul prayed his father would do as he was told. He became aware of himself beseeching God to let his father just empty the till. He felt himself shake.

The man by the door was becoming frantic. 'Just take the fucking till.'

Now Abdul wondered if he could help his father. His phone was in his pocket. He did not dare move to take it out.

Finally, Tarek's fear melted. He called through:

'Abdul, call the police...'

Before he could finish, the bat disrupted his shout. A blow to the head; Tarek's arms were not fast enough to deflect the blow. Abdul heard his father fall against the shelves. He heard the bat strike, three, four times more.

The man by the door had reached a frenzy:

'You said he was on his fucking own. Grab the shit and let's go.'

Abdul heard all this. He acted. He acted in a way that he would always feel ashamed of. He crept the few inches to the door, and locked it with a shaking hand. His panicked mind calculated that he should keep himself safe. Hearing the robbery in the shop, he knelt and then sat on the floor. Every inch of him begged not to be noticed. He pulled out his phone, but hesitated. He thought about dialling a number. He could barely hold the phone still.

He heard the bat swinging against his father at least six times. The robbers, in a frenzy, yelled racial insults, beating the ageing man mercilessly and unrelentingly. He heard them spit. He heard the till being broken open, he heard shelves being cleared and he heard the shop being trashed. Abdul's fear escalated when, once, the door to the store room was bumped. Then he heard the door to the shop open and close. Then there was silence.

Abdul still did not move. He still breathed deeply and quietly. His eyes were wet with tears. The phone, undialled, remained in his shaking hands. He felt a lump in his throat, and his body was saturated with fear. Finally, he moved, slowly, gradually, and unlocked the storeroom door.

The first sight to hit him was the mess in the shop. The goods and products were scattered; in their rage the robbers had left nothing in its place.

Underneath the dislodged till, wedged behind the counter, lay Tarek. This sight fell on Abdul like the bat that had immobilised his father. He was battered and bloody. His father's face bled from unknown wounds; his shirt was saturated with blood; scattered over his body were the letters from the bank. Abdul always remembered the unnatural way his father lay. He did not look peaceful or resting; it looked like he had been wedged forcefully into the gap behind the counter.

Abdul just stared. He felt nauseous.

He heard sirens. Despite his own inaction, his mother in the flat upstairs had heard the noise and called the police. The neighbour in the flat next door had done the same.

From this point, everything was a blur. First police then paramedics arrived, and he stood there. He was taken aside and spoken to by the police. He remembered speaking to them, but couldn't remember what he said. Then his mother was at the door of the shop, tears on her face visible in the dim light. Her face was in her hands as Tarek was bundled into an ambulance. Abdul would always remember her crying. He had never seen her sob before.

In the stress of the situation, Abdul acted on impulse. Had he been asked to document what had happened since the attack, he would have offered the vaguest of summaries.

His sense of time was altered. Everything seemed to take an eternity, but he had the sensation of moving quickly. Before he knew it he was on his way to the hospital. Soon he was sitting in the waiting area. The environment was sterile and quiet. It was much brighter than the shop with its strong artificial light and white décor. Next to him sat his mother. Her face was swollen, and at times she still sobbed. The two had not spoken since leaving the shop; they had handed keys to the police and travelled by taxi. Now they waited. They did not know what was happening with Tarek. They just waited.

Ibrahim arrived. He sat on the other side of his mother. He was shaken but tried to appear calm. He made the appropriate noises: he asked what was happening with his father. He said that he was disgusted by how vile people could be, that he knew his father was a strong man and would pull through. Ibrahim was much more twitchy than the other two. He moved around a lot, pacing at times and rubbing his face.

Abdul remained still and silent. He did not even know what he thought. He lacked even the mental capacity to hope that his father would be all right. He sat on the uncomfortable chair, without even the presence of mind to move his back to a more comfortable position. To look at him, you would wonder if he had undergone hypnosis.

He became aware of Ibrahim talking to him.

'You all right, bro?'

He looked at Ibrahim, who was sitting down, leaning past the sobbing Awet to look at Abdul.

'You all right, bro?' repeated Ibrahim.

'Yeah, fine.'

He noticed that his mother had turned to look at him as well. He wondered why she looked at him like that. He struggled to read her expression, her face was swollen from the sobbing. He tried to process what she may be thinking. Was it sympathy or judgement on her face?

'What did the police say? Did you see the people, Abdul?' asked Ibrahim.

Abdul's suspicion of his mother exploded into outright paranoia. Questions and doubts about his family filled his thoughts. He knew they were judging him; he knew that they knew he had done nothing. That while his father was being beaten he had sat there, afraid and pathetic. He judged himself for it, and he knew that they judged him for it. His mind went from agreeing with his family's judgement to anger that they were questioning him. He made excuses for his behaviour to himself. They were aggressive men and intent on the robbery. He would have just ended up like his father. However fair, he did not truly believe this.

'No, I didn't,' he answered bluntly. He hoped they would just leave him alone with his guilt.

'As long as you're OK. It must've been awful.'

Awet muttered agreement. She innocently reached out and held Abdul's hand.

'It would be awful if you were there as well,' she said sincerely.

These sentiments enraged Abdul as he sat there, still ostensibly emotionless. His paranoid impulses told him that this show of care was just a lie. They just wanted to make him feel safe, so he would explain his patheticness. He felt that they were judging him. He knew they thought he was pathetic, the boy who had not even been able to call the police. He did not feel he deserved his mother's affection. His mind retched.

After a moment, he responded adversely to his mother's touch. In as controlled a manner as possible, he rose; he attempted to appear calm, though anyone who watched him would see an emotionally torn boy. His face was strained with stress. Arms folded awkwardly, he wouldn't even make eye contact. He focused on the wall then the floor, whichever seemed to judge him less. Staring at the wall again, he declared he needed some air, and was out of the waiting room before his family could even breathe to stop him.

Fleeing his family's guilt-ridden affection, escaping the oppressive waiting room, he hurried through the corridors of the hospital. He passed visitors and patients, some as anxious-looking as his own family. Finally, he went out into the night, breathing the cold air.

He made his way onto backstreets, appreciating the quiet emptiness. Even when a sound did break the silence, Abdul was hardly able to notice it. His pace was fast as he drifted through the dimly lit streets towards his home.

He was desperate to calm his mind. As he walked he began to detach himself from his thoughts. Away from the emotionally charged scene of the hospital, he was able to push back the memory of the attack. He tried to convince himself there was nothing he could have done.

There *was* nothing he could have done. He could not have defended his father. He was no match for two armed men. His reaction in that situation was to succumb to a natural and awful fear. It was the vilest experience of his life.

Logical thought was not so easy. His families' emotions were like fuel to the guilt that burned in his mind. No matter how clear it was that Abdul had not let anyone down, he wished he had been able to do something. To fight against the hate that had destroyed his father. The guilt-drenched part of his mind still taunted him that he was a coward; there had never been such a pathetic son.

As he walked, these thoughts became less persistent. As he reached the shop his feet carried him, he was hardly in any control of their direction. They didn't take him to the flat, rather to the door of the shop. Then he stopped. Across the slightly opened door was a police cordon. There was a police car still parked on the street, but he could see no one around.

He wanted to go into the shop. He could feel his muscles pushing him to pass under the barrier and through the open door. He had enough presence of mind not to do this. Instead he stood at the shop window, looking into the dark shop, only dimly lit by the light of the fridges. He looked hard towards the counter at the end of the shop. He stood, imagining his father still lying there. The image of his father's blood-soaked clothes was stapled to Abdul's mind. Tears streamed down his face.

He didn't know why he had come here. He was acting only on impulse.

As he stared into the gloom of the shop, ten then fifteen minutes swept by before he became aware of himself and his circumstances: his father beaten by racists, now in hospital, a mother traumatised and an incapable brother. Then there was him.

His father's attack wounded Abdul much deeper. When faced with adversity he did not know how to act; he felt weak.

Abdul's hurt was deeper still. Though distant, Tarek had always been a stable figure in his life. The sudden display of Tarek's impermanence showed Abdul how that which seemed most stable could disappear in an instant. For the first time he contemplated the fragility of his own life and circumstances.

Chapter Eight

Dawn squeezed the tea bag with her spoon and removed it from the cup. She stirred three sugars into the boiling water, then one more for luck, dropped in the milk and carried it over to the table.

'Here you go,' she said as she placed the tea in front of Darren. She smiled her broad, endearing smile as she sat down with him.

'Thanks, Nan,' said Darren, wrapping his hand around the cup.

'More biscuits?' asked Dawn, pushing the plate in front of him.

'Thanks,' he said, leaning over to the table to take a sixth chocolate digestive.

The late afternoon sun was shining through the window. Since his first time in this house it had hardly changed. It was tired, cluttered with old pictures covering the walls, with the same worn carpets; Darren would not want this house to change. He came here when he could, and always felt better for it.

In her home, which was best described as her habitat, Dawn had grown older. She still dyed her hair, but more infrequently. The grey roots could be seen growing through. Her face was more pale and wrinkled, showing the signs of a lifetime of stress and worry. Her loving character however remained undiminished by age.

'I didn't expect you today, Darren, love,' said Dawn, speaking more slowly than she used to. 'Did school finish early?'

Darren nodded, not making eye contact. Both knew that he should be in school on this Friday afternoon. She guessed he had at least attended in the morning as he was sitting in his school uniform.

'And how's your mum today?'

'She's OK, I think. I saw her yesterday but I haven't seen her today.'

Dawn tutted. A large proportion of the wrinkles etched on her face could be attributed to her worries about her daughter Jane. Her mental health changed so frequently. Dawn used to visit Jane when she could, but her walking had become much worse with age. It was rare for Jane to visit her parents.

She asked some more questions about Jane. What she had been doing, whether she was going out. To her relief, Darren said that his mother was quite active at the moment. She was attending the doctor again and seemed on top of things. Dawn was glad. There had been a month or so last year when Jane had hardly left her bedroom. Dawn had been taking food round to Darren some days and checking the state of the flat while Jane festered in her depression.

Sitting with Darren, Dawn sprung into a story about Jane when she was young. She remembered fondly their first holiday, a long weekend at the sea when Jane was twelve. Darren listened quietly. He enjoyed hearing about his mother when she was young, and found listening to his grandmother very calming. He was also tired, so was happy to sit and listen without the need to interact.

Dawn finished her story and looked over at Darren.

'Listen to me going on like an old lady!' she said. 'I'll put the telly on.'

The two of them moved into the living room with tea and more biscuits. A daytime quiz show was on the TV, which Dawn found gripping. Darren, bemused, watched her get animated and wound up. She supported random people she did not know, guessing they were decent people from just looking at them. She was genuinely upset when a meek young girl got a question about politics wrong.

'Come on, love, it was easy!' she shouted at the TV. It was at this moment that Darren's grandfather returned home.

'Hullo,' his gruff voice rumbled through the house as he entered.

Before he even entered the room, Dawn was on her feet. She asked him abruptly:

'Frank, you'll never guess what question this woman just got wrong. What was Tony Benn's middle name?'

Frank was entering the room, having removed his coat. He was not perturbed by Dawn being so wound up, he half expected it at this time of day.

'Mr Tony Benn,' said Frank, happy for a question about one of his favourite politicians. 'It was Wedgewood.'

'See,' said Dawn triumphantly. 'Everyone knows.'

Darren was a bit bewildered by his grandmother's animation. She disappeared to the kitchen to get a cup of tea for her husband. She also needed to calm down after her new favourite contestant who had ever entered a quiz show got a simple question wrong.

Frank entered the living room and noticed Darren.

'Hullo, young man, nice to see you!'

Darren beamed and smiled at his granddad. Frank sat in the armchair opposite the TV; the chair was so accustomed to supporting Frank's figure it was perfectly moulded to the shape of his body. Darren noticed his grandfather's socks; his big toes stuck out of both, as if they were purposefully knitted not to cover the toe. He leant down and put his slippers on.

'How was school, then?'

Frank was completely unaware that school was still on and that Darren should still have been there. He had gone through his life 'just going with it'. If Darren was in his house at 2.30pm on a Friday afternoon in his school uniform, that's just the way it was. He wasn't the sort of person that worried about details.

'It was OK,' replied Darren. He hated school and hated talking about it.

'I didn't like school much at your age. Couldn't wait to leave at fourteen, get working, earning some money, causing trouble with the union,' he smiled.

'Yeah,' said Darren.

Frank was very intelligent. He had not learnt things at school but picked up knowledge through his working life. He had started reading books at thirty.

'Yeah, but it's not like that now. You stay till you're sixteen and then where do you work?'

Darren shrugged.

Frank made some disparaging remarks about Thatcher and the Tory government of the 1980s. He made the point that the country had been better in the 1960s and 1970s, with more work, more manufacturing and more self-respect for the working man ('and woman!' he added quickly). Then he returned to Darren and his lack of prospects.

'There must be something you like though, Darren?'

'Well, I like sport – football and stuff.'

'Good lad! You look athletic!'

Darren smiled. He hoped people would notice he wasn't like the fat kids in his school.

'You think about what you'll do after school? What are you good at?'

'I'm rubbish at school.'

Frank didn't know what to say. He did value education, despite having hated school himself.

'I know it's hard, Darren,' said Frank slowly, knowing he was supposed to say something like this to encourage the young boy. This made Darren feel awkward. 'I know it's hard,' he said again. 'But if you can do well now it will be easier when you leave. Do you think about what you'll do? You like sport?'

'I was thinking about the army. Cos I like exercise and you can learn skills and stuff. Would be better than school.'

Frank was quiet for a second. He was a little disappointed.

'They kill people as well, Darren,' Frank stated bluntly. He continued quickly, 'But I had a thought the other day. A friend of mine could sort you some work experience in his store just down the road here. What do you think?'

Before Darren could answer they heard the phone ring, then Dawn having a short conversation in the kitchen. Then she hurried into the living room.

'Darren, that was your mum. The school was on and she's really worried about you. Get yourself home. The next bus is in twenty minutes, so you'll have to run.'

Darren grabbed his bag from the floor and headed towards the front door. Before he left Frank called him back and shoved ten pounds into his hand.

Arriving at the bus stop just as the bus was coming, Darren dived on it and sat on the top deck. The bus took over an hour, so he got comfy on the back seat, sprawled out. He felt a bit guilty about worrying his mum, but the school didn't usually notice when he wasn't there. He knew that Mum would be panicking until he got home, so he resolved to get there as soon as possible. He drifted into a light sleep.

The bus pulled into the centre of Milltown, and he had a ten-minute walk to his estate. He passed some shops then turned into the estate of terraces that preceded his block. Milltown had a peculiar feel at this time of day. It was always busy and full of people wandering around. Darren sometimes felt uncomfortable when he passed groups of strangers outside the pubs.

As he reached his block he noticed a group of young people in the communal gardens. As he came closer he realised he knew them all. His focus was drawn to the scruffy and aggressive young girl who he remembered pushing the Muslim boy a few weeks ago. He had not seen her for a while. Today she was louder than ever, and her behaviour more disorderly. He could hear her loud and shrill cackle as he approached.

One of the crowd shouted to him as he approached:

'Ey up, Darren!'

Darren nodded to them.

'Not seen you in a time, where you been?'

'Here and there,' he said, too embarrassed to admit that he had bunked off school to spend an afternoon with his grandparents.

Today about seven people were gathered. All seemed fairly subdued, except for the girl. She oppressed them with her exaggerated behaviour. She was even more full of life than usual; even as Darren was greeting people in the group, he could hear her loudly in the background. Her laugh was offensive to his ears.

Darren was not talkative today. He wanted to get back to see his mum.

The girl caught sight of Darren.

'He don't know yet, do he?' she said as she saw him. She leapt over to him, smiling a triumphant grin as she approached. Darren took note of her teeth. Even though she was young, they were a mess. Some were black and one of the front ones was badly chipped.

'Don't know what?' asked Darren. He was not enthusiastic about hearing what she had to say. She was not the type to be excited by anything pleasant.

When he spoke to her he made a point of looking at her and not changing his own behaviour. He hated watching those around him looking down and avoiding her when she spoke.

'Well...' she said. At this moment she stood on a bench to elevate herself above everyone. 'You know that Paki shop what got done the other week? With that quiet kid what works there,' she said, looking down on her audience.

He had heard about the attack in school. Darren also couldn't easily forget the young Muslim boy she had pushed over. His petrified and innocent face was etched onto his mind. The news had made him feel nauseous.

'Yeah,' he replied, wanting this interaction to be over.

'Well...'

She was not going to pass this information on quickly, savouring the attention she gleaned.

'Well... turns out the attacker was Benny, my mum's brother,' she stated. 'He fucking showed that Paki cunt!' she added. She spewed malice with every word.

'Thought all your family was all inside,' said Darren, trying not to react too much to this news despite it making his stomach turn.

'So did I, I ain't seen him in ages, but when Mum called the other night, she said she'd seen in the paper that it was him, cos she recognised him in the picture. Only just out and already putting Paki twats back in their place.'

He hated her gloating. He could not show that he was being provoked, but he could not find it in him to condone what she was describing. He nodded and then turned to one of his closer friends.

'Do you still do that boxing?' he asked him. 'Could I come with you again one week?'

Realising she had lost her audience, the girl turned to another member of the group and faded into Darren's peripheral vision.

'Course – I'll ask my dad later.'

'Cool. I'll call round tomorrow, then, and see what he says.'

The boy nodded in agreement.

'I gotta go, anyway,' said Darren, and quickly wandered over to his block.

He let himself in and began ascending the stairs. As he rose he reflected on the day. He was more resolved than ever that he needed to do something when he left school. He wanted to make money to support his mother and he did not want to be hanging round, like some of his older peers. Moreover, he wanted to be away from people like the aggressive girl outside. He wanted to join the army. Until he was sixteen and old enough to join, he was going to make himself as fit and healthy as possible.

He entered their flat to a flustered mother.

*

That evening, while Darren was managing a manic mother, Awet was on the phone. She sat on the old sofa, facing a wall in dire need of being painted, talking to Ibrahim. Like her two daughters, he had been calling every day. As Ibrahim lived so close, he had also been doing bits of work in the shop, which the family couldn't afford to close. This had allowed Awet to visit Tarek in the hospital. Abdul's two sisters had visited earlier in the week though neither had stayed long.

The living room was dimly lit and the light overhead occasionally flickered.

Abdul was not in the living room. He was in his bedroom, which directly connected to the living room. He could hear the conversation.

'Yes, I spoke to them; they say maybe in two weeks they will come over again.'

Ibrahim made a comment suggesting his sisters should be doing more.

'It's not that easy, Ibrahim. If they lose their work we would only have the shop. We need everyone doing as much as possible for the family.'

Ibrahim changed to asking about Tarek.

'He was much better today, I have to say. He was talking a lot of sense, and he was less tired. The doctor was happy with him as well...'

Another interruption from Ibrahim, then:

'They did not say how long before he is home. They still think that his memory may be a problem. They keep doing mental tests. He still has concentration, but he is struggling with the logic and memory ones.'

There was silence again as Ibrahim spoke.

'That's great. It will give me a bit of time at the hospital tomorrow.'

Another silence. Awet's voice became more muffled and Abdul could not hear what she was saying. This was happening on most of her phone calls and Abdul knew she was discussing him. He had initially just listened more attentively. After a few phone calls he was bored of hearing the same short-sighted analysis of his behaviour: Awet was happy that Abdul had given up college to work in the shop, but didn't know how to show she was grateful; she noticed that he was even more quiet than ever; he hardly even looked at her; he seemed to be on auto-pilot, drifting from his bedroom to work and back. When she tried to communicate with him, there was nothing. He would not spend a moment longer with her than he had to.

Abdul's bedroom was lit only by the glow of his laptop. The dark reflected his mood. He had never been full of life, always being shy and reserved. Any social energy he had possessed had been doused by his school life. After he witnessed his father's attack, it was as if the last embers of a fire had been stamped out. Inside, he felt no will, no need to speak to anyone. He didn't feel that anyone would care should he decide to try and interact; he hardly even acknowledged his own thoughts. He was drifting through his life, dominated by misery and self-pity, driven by nothing more than a vague idea of what a son was expected to do.

He had been to the hospital once. He did not care to see his father debilitated. Abdul's thoughts were no longer consumed by guilt. There was instead a disengaged emptiness.

Awet, who sat so alone each night in the living room, thinking about her husband and desperate to help her son, wondered what Abdul did on his own. Many things crossed her mind. She knew he liked reading, and hoped perhaps he was trying to keep on top of studies for when he could go back to college. She knew this was optimistic. She thought perhaps he watched films on his laptop, to distract himself from the bleakness of his life. Perhaps he even had a porn-watching habit.

Awet did not even get close to what Abdul was up to. Alone, with just a laptop and the internet, he had found some dark materials to engage with. His obsession actually had roots from before his father was attacked. One evening, having been working in the shop, he had been watching the news with his father. There had been an Islamic extremist arrested for inciting hate. This had whetted Abdul's interest in an academic way. He was interested in what kind of Islam this man preached. Previously Abdul had only ever heard calm, peace-loving clerics in the mosque. Now he was interested in how his religion could be used for hate.

Of course he had been aware of the passages in the Qur'an about infidels and unbelievers. Yet he had met few clerics who had paid attention to these passages; religions had developed in different times and this had to be kept in mind. One preacher he remembered had taken this subject head on. He had explained that the infidels in the Qur'an meant those making war against Muslims when the Qur'an was written. This meant violent pagans in Mecca and did not mean all non-believers; the Qur'an had been written in a violent time, after all. In fact, the passages specifically called for peace except against those who made war on you. He had always been taught that Muslims only fight in self-defence, that peace and non-violence were the principal ways of Muslims.

He had read briefly about the Muslims who had declared a Jihad, who were apparently hell-bent on killing all non-believers. He had not taken much more notice than this.

Since his father was in hospital, he had begun looking into more extreme Islamic propaganda. At this moment, he was still not completely convinced by it, but the messages it contained seemed to kindle something in his otherwise emotionally empty life. The anger and the passion moved him in his dishevelled state.

While Awet muttered quietly on the phone, Abdul was reading an essay about Islam. Written by an extremist preacher based in the UK, it covered the need for an Islamic state, to protect Muslims from the enemies it faced. Abdul read the impassioned call to create an Islamic caliphate; he felt his heart beating as he read the conclusion:

Islam is under attack globally. We are under attack. Just look each day at the news. Just look at the white soldiers patrolling our streets, in Iraq, in Afghanistan, in the Muslim world. They seek any fake, pathetic reason to land their armed men on our soil, to trash our way of life, to trash our homeland, to smash our people. They drop their bombs like cowards on our people. They drive their tanks and their trucks onto our soil. And who will be next? Where will be next? Iran? Sudan? Libya? The American dogs seek to debilitate Islam wherever they can.

(I have not even mentioned the humiliation they put our Muslims through in their countries. Muslims who were dragged to the West to serve their economies, then degraded by racism each day. I will cover this in a future essay.)

There is only one conclusion. There can only be one conclusion. We need an Islamic State. A homeland for Muslims everywhere. A strong and unyielding state, where Muslims live as brothers, where Muslim law reigns, where we are safe from the attacks of the West. Where we are strong and safe from war.

Islam is peace. But we must defend ourselves from the attacks of our enemies. We cannot have peace when we are subject to endless attacks. Do not think that we are not at war. We are. We have been for centuries. We need a state. We must defend the brotherhood of Islam. We need Muslims to fight together as one.

Abdul read these words and sat back in his chair. The whole essay had engaged him. He had never read before, in one place, how much violence there had been in the Middle East. He had never recognised that land as being his homeland, nor thought about the violence targeting only Muslims. He had never before thought of this in terms of a battle, that Muslims were being attacked by outside enemies. He began to see himself as a Muslim in a wider sense. He felt a camaraderie with those afflicted by violence.

Abdul looked over the essay again. He wanted to know more about this writer. He wanted to learn more about injustice; each time he read an essay like this he felt something. A rare spark of emotion in an emotionally void life. The idea of a community of Islam started to mean something to him. No longer did he feel that being a Muslim just meant going to a mosque once a week. He began to see himself as part of an oppressed people.

He looked over the essay for the name of the writer, for the area he lived in, anything that would allow him to find more. He was not stupid. He knew that extremists wouldn't go putting their addresses online for the authorities to find them. He was also sure, on the other hand, that anyone writing this would want people to get in touch. They wanted members.

There was a name on the essay. Probably an alias, but that was something to go off. He searched. Starting with legitimate search engines, then delving into the darker areas of the web, he searched out the author of this work.

He found more essays under the same name, more calls to arms for Muslims. Little else, however, was attached to these words. No clue as to who the writer may be.

He was going to give up. Tiredness and disappointment weighed heavily on him. He made one more search and rooted through some more essays, all by the same named author.

Then his heart started to beat faster. He shook off the tiredness. One article displayed a picture of a closed mosque looking like it had been damaged in a raid. The sign outside was still visible and it displayed a phone number, curiously a UK number. Abdul wrote it down.

He resolved to ring the next day. He knew that he needed sleep, that he was restless, and that he may think differently in the morning.

He put his laptop screen down and turned to his single bed. Taking off his clothes, he realised how tired he was. He considered going to the bathroom to brush his teeth, but didn't want to pass his mother in the living room. He decided to wash thoroughly in the morning. He climbed into bed, his mind going over the idea of calling these people, his brothers.

He lay there; thoughts flooded into his head and prevented sleep. Over and over, the ideas he had read travelled through his mind. The essay told him he was not British, he was a Muslim. He contemplated the idea that he was part of a people under attack. He nurtured the idea that he may have a role in defending his people.

Perhaps the strongest draw of this idea was that it gave him an escape from his current rut. Before reading this material, his only option seemed to be to spend his life slaving away in a shop in a hostile town, caring for a disabled father with a family who seemed disinterested; now he could imagine himself as a soldier.

Suddenly he jumped out of bed. He breathed deeply, almost hyperventilating. He knew he wanted to call. He would call now.

He dived across the dark room and grabbed the phone on his desk. He steadied himself as he held the phone before entering the number. Then he paused. He briefly thought about his family, what they may say or think about him now. He pushed them out of his head. An emotion he had never felt before drove him to act; it was an emotion that overpowered any feeling of family ties.

He pressed the eleven digits into the phone and put it to his ear. It was ringing.

Chapter Nine

Abdul alighted the bus. It was cold but light; the cool winter sun shone through the windows of the bus station and he could see his breath. Entering the bus station, he looked around. He felt nervous and tense. He breathed deeply through his nose and slowly took in his environment. Each step he took was filled with doubt.

The three-hour bus journey had been one of constant debate. What was he doing? Why was he going? Would his family see through his paper-thin lie excusing his absence?

He found a bench beneath a poster in the station. The bus had arrived ten minutes early, so he guessed they may not be here. Sitting down, he pulled up the hood of his jumper and looked down as he had been instructed. He waited.

Five then ten minutes passed. All the while the debate whirled in his head. He knew he could still get away, escape. He felt a twitch in his leg as part of his mind tried to move him. But a greater part made him stay. His whole life he could not remember doing anything that made him feel so nervous yet so excited. Never had he been so torn. The logical part of him reasoned that he should not be here; something deeper held him in place. It was an unnamed feeling. He did not feel properly in control of himself. He couldn't even say that fifty percent of his body wanted to be there; the part that did held him in place firmly. He was like a ship anchored in a storm, winds pulling him in all directions, but staying where he was.

He waited for the stranger he had spoken to a handful of times on the phone. He didn't even know for certain that this person would turn up.

His logical mind pointed to his family. He felt guilty about the burden his absence was putting on them. Leaving Milltown meant his mother and Ibrahim working in the shop as well as caring for his father.

This was also one of the reasons he was so determined to leave today. The daily grind of the shop, the same daily tasks in the same order, the same impersonal experiences with the same customers, were making him ill. He wanted to be away from his family. He was sick of Ibrahim trying to be nice on those days he did manage to come and help, or his sisters and their supportive phone calls. He was sick of his mother's obvious exhaustion and her constant leaning on him. He was sick of his father, now returned home, sitting in an armchair, immobile, speechless and depressed. He was sick of looking at his father's face, scarred from the attack.

Today was the first day that Abdul had not been in the shop or flat for three months.

He shivered slightly as he waited. Head down and hood up, he sat quietly, staring at the floor. He was tired. He had been on the bus since 5 a.m.

Two worn-out black trainers appeared in front of him. Abdul noticed the faded black tracksuit over the trainers. He looked up. A young man stood above Abdul. He was slightly obscured by shadow caused by the sun directly behind him. Abdul looked at him, struck by how different he appeared to how he imagined. The man on the end of the phone had been so eloquent and wise. He had imagined someone much older.

Instead there was a young, thin, shabbily dressed man before him, staring at him intently. He had a serious look on his face, assessing Abdul. He looked away from the figure's face. He noticed in his hand he was holding a woollen hat.

'Abdul?' he asked.

Abdul nodded. 'Adam?'

The stranger nodded once.

'Come this way.'

He led him through the main exit of the bus station and into a small car park on a backstreet. Abdul only passively noticed the town. He saw small red-brick buildings and terraces. Empty and tired-looking shops were interspersed among the structures.

They stopped at a car. A large man sat in the driver's seat. Adam opened the back door and signalled for Abdul to get in. He then followed Abdul through the same door, pushing him into the middle seat. He turned to look intensely at Abdul.

'We don't know you, so we don't trust you. Trust is earned.'

He then slowly pulled the woollen hat over Abdul's face; his vision was restricted. He pushed Abdul down, so he lay awkwardly over the back seat. Adam's arm remained gently on his shoulder.

Blindfolded, his fate now out of his hands, Abdul felt strangely less nervous. As there was nothing he could do now to get away, he just accepted what would happen. Inside he stopped worrying and debating. Any possible choice he previously had was now gone. The arm on his shoulder made him feel secure. There was no going back.

He felt the car moving through the streets. His two new companions were silent.

After an unknown amount of time, the car made a number of turns. Abdul heard the engine's low hum as the speed reduced. Finally he felt the power of the reverse gear pull the car backwards. The car stopped, the engine went off, and for a moment there was silence.

His head was still covered by the woollen hat, which was uncomfortably warm from his breath. The stillness of the car slowly increased his anxiety again. He would be plunged even deeper into the unknown.

Adam's arm slowly pulled Abdul up. The car door opened and he was guided out of the back seat. Abdul squinted as a hand removed the hat and his eyes became re-accustomed to the light. He was standing in front of a brick wall in a cobbled alleyway. The passage was long but felt claustrophobic.

Slightly to the right was a wooden gate. It was wedged tight into the brickwork and Adam wrestled to open it. He then came and stood uncomfortably close to Abdul. He indicated to him to pass through.

As he moved, the car drove away.

Through the gate he found himself in a small concrete yard. Before him he saw the back of a row of terraced houses. The house in front of him had a small single-storey extension at the back. Abdul saw the guttering was hanging broken on the wall.

Before he could take in any more he was prodded forward. The wooden door to the house was slightly open and he was guided inside. Directly beyond the door was a room to the right, which Abdul noted was a toilet, and dark staircase to the left. The staircase had clearly not been decorated since the house was built. Wallpaper peeled from the walls and there was no carpet covering the wooden stairs. The only light in the space came from the open door below; this disappeared as Adam closed the door.

Abdul slowly made his way upwards. His footsteps on the creaking staircase seemed loud as he ascended. He could make out a little light leaking from another door at the top. He felt each beat of his heart as he approached.

When Abdul reached the final stair, feeling Adam's presence directly behind him, the door opened. Abdul tried to take in everything before him while being paralysed by self-consciousness.

The room was half full. There were maybe eight people there. He quickly looked them over. The person who had opened the door was the most striking. A large man of presumably African origin dressed completely in black stood imposingly at the door. He had the most serious face Abdul had ever seen, wrinkled and scarred; Abdul couldn't even imagine what a smile might look like on this face. One eye was noticeably more closed than the other.

Abdul glanced away from him to the others in the room. The rest were all male and less likely to stand out in a crowd. Three, he noticed, were well presented and dressed in shirts. He was drawn to the man he presumed to be the Imam. He was the only one sitting on the floor, a serious look on his bearded face. He frowned slightly and seemed to be mentally elsewhere, staring at the book opened before him. While the rest of the room had turned to see the newcomers, the Imam had not even moved. It was difficult to say why, but he appeared approachable. Abdul took a liking to this inoffensive and kind-looking man.

The room itself was lit only by one light hanging in the centre. Aside from the people in the room there was nothing. No furniture, no wallpaper, nothing. It was defined by its emptiness. The window was boarded up, making it feel like it was night time outside. The creaking floorboards were covered by a mat. There was, he noticed, a very small structure halfway up one of the walls; from the decoration he guessed this to be a mihrab.

As he was standing in the doorway a hand landed forcefully on his shoulder.

'Remove your shoes.'

It was the voice of the large man by the door. The order was delivered in a gruff whisper. Abdul obliged.

He was guided into the room by Adam. He was aware of everyone looking at him. As he passed the tall doorman he nodded his head, to which the doorman offered a frown. The door was closed and the large man stood, arms folded, before it. His legs were slightly apart, in an almost military pose. Abdul was thankful to have Adam with him, who took the initiative. He pulled him forward to the Imam on the floor, while all the others in the room silently watched.

'This is the new one,' said Adam.

'Good,' replied the elderly man without moving. 'And what do you think of him?'

'He talked a good talk on the phone, but we'll see.'

Now the elderly man looked up. He smiled at Abdul. Until this point he had been standing rigid, not wanting to move in case he caused offence to his new company. As the elderly man smiled, he felt himself loosen. Though he wanted to, he did not smile back; he was too self-conscious to move even his lips.

'Welcome to our little mosque,' said the old man kindly. 'It's not much, but the size of a mosque is not based on the number of bricks in the walls, but on the strength of the faith of its members.'

Abdul half-smiled at this. He felt a glimmer of pride. He had faith, and he felt strong being around others who shared that faith. He stole another look at the man guarding the door.

'He is a very loyal man, the most loyal. He will be loyal to you, if you prove faithful, or he will be hell if not.'

Abdul nodded, slightly embarrassed that his glance had been noticed. There was a slight change on the face of the man by the door. A look of satisfaction crept across his creased face.

The elderly Imam looked at his watch. 'We always start with prayers. Then we will discuss the struggle.'

The men in the room assembled into a line along the floor and prayers began. The group, as one, genuflected and bowed in the direction of the mihrab. Abdul was positioned next to Adam at the far end of the line. He saw how small the space was. The line of men hardly fitted in across the room and there was little space for a second line behind them.

When the brief religious observance was over the Imam called them to sit with him. The group, except the man who returned to standing by the door, formed a semi-circle around the Imam.

For a moment there was silence. He had returned to the book positioned in front of him. Abdul took the opportunity to survey the audience more closely.

Everyone included, there were ten people in the room. In the sitting group, all except one were around his age. The older man in the group looked about fifty and was nondescript. Sitting directly opposite Abdul were two men who he felt were similar to him. They were dressed in a similar way and did not look tidy; their hair needed washing and their clothes looked worn-out. The final three people interested Abdul the most. They were professional-looking young men, dressed as if they had just left a solicitor's office. They looked wealthy. Their clean shirts appeared brand new and the three of them had ostentatious watches on their wrists. More than this, they looked arrogant. It was difficult to point to exactly what made them appear like this: possibly it was their eyes, or some nuance in their expressions.

At length the Imam talked:

'Friends, nothing pleases me more than to see our numbers growing. Just last week we welcomed John to our little mosque, and now this week we welcome Abdul.'

Saying this, he indicated the fifty-year-old man and Abdul. John looked rigid and nervous as well; Abdul could empathise with how he felt. Unlike Abdul, he did smile at the group as he was introduced.

The Imam continued:

'As the horrors in our homelands come to light, there will be a growing Muslim awakening. More and more will want to join the fight with our brothers abroad. But we must be vigilant. As our movement grows, so too will police interest in our activities. We will take every precaution with new members. We can never be too careful when it comes to security and we cannot give our trust away quickly.'

At these words, Abdul noticed the large man by the door staring intently at him. He was almost snarling. These comments had a deflating impact on Abdul. It hammered home that in this group he would be a suspect until he could prove himself; yet by being here he was making himself a pariah to the British state. He felt alone and daunted by the effort needed to be included here.

'Now, I am sorry I am speaking English,' continued the Imam. 'But it is sadly the language we all share. So many people now from our homeland do not speak our language, the language of the prophet, of the Qur'an. I have heard that there are mosques now in Britain which don't even do prayers in Arabic. I have heard there are children who think that Mohammed spoke English. I have heard that some Muslim children now can't even name the land that their families come from, thinking they have always lived in Britain.'

There was a look of disgust on the face of the Imam.

'Indeed, they want us to forget our history, because then we forget who we are. They want us to learn their language and *assimilate*. They want us to forget our culture, our background, our heritage. But we do not forget our history. We know that they, the Western powers, invaded and occupied our lands. We know they forced our people to come here and work in their economies, using us to work and make their countries rich. We know that we are not part of this society and we know we will never be accepted here.'

He looked around the room. He pointed to one of the men in shirts.

'Tell us about your family, your roots. Where are you from?'

The arrogant man did not hesitate and spoke naturally, as if he had been waiting for the moment.

'My family and I are from Iraq. They left in the early nineties after the American invasion. Because of the trouble stirred up by the Americans, my family were persecuted in our homeland.'

'You see, this is what we mean. They went in with their planes and tanks, saying they will help Kuwait, but did nothing. Then they left, and they left behind a mess. Leaving Muslims attacking Muslims. Of course, the real problem in Iraq was caused by the British. They took it in their empire and broke the Muslim rule that had been there. It happened in 1921, they set up their own little kingdom, the Hashemite kingdom, and ignored the wishes of the Muslims in the land. They were subjected to British rule, and no true, independent Muslim state has existed there since. The problems there now are caused by the imperial powers, who keep ravaging it for resources.'

The young man who had spoken was nodding enthusiastically. Tears were in his eyes.

'And what did your parents do?'

'My father was a doctor, he worked in the hospital here for ten years before his death.'

'You see,' exclaimed the Imam triumphantly. 'Not only do they conduct their wars, they take our trained people in the aftermath of their attacks. They bring our doctors here to look after British people, when our people need doctors too!'

Abdul was overwhelmed. He had never known such a strong sense of community. He felt a deep sense of belonging here with people who had a shared history and a shared cause. This was the first time he had been in the presence of people who identified as Muslim in this way. It was not about going to the mosque, it was about being part of a people.

He was embarrassed too. His ignorance of Muslim history made him feel inadequate. He had limited knowledge of the history of Iraq or other Muslim states. It did occur to him that he was being told a very specific narrative designed by the Imam. The history of these areas was far more complicated than the Imam suggested. He was also upset as he couldn't recount his own family history. He knew that his family came from the Middle East, but exactly which country, he did not know. He believed it was Palestine, but he couldn't be certain. There was a family story about his grandfather working with the British army and coming to Britain because of this.

These were the feelings that the Imam wanted to instil. As he spoke, he wanted the young men to feel there was a knowledge, a truth, that he could enlighten them to. He used his history to ensnare the young and easily influenced. History bears no objective narrative and here it was a recruitment tool, used to colour and disfigure the malleable views of those gathered.

The Imam was still talking. Abdul felt he was approaching his conclusion:

'From the imperial age to now, our homelands have only ever known occupation and oppression. Just look at the states there now. Saudi Arabia, which bows to any whim of its American paymasters. The state of Iraq, which is undoubtedly just another American satellite state, with the government they imposed. I do not need to draw your attention to the issues in Palestine, caused by America's support for Israel. Then there is Syria, upheld and defended by Russia. I cannot think of a country in these areas that is not dominated by the new imperial powers. How can Muslims have self-respect if we do not even have an independent homeland?'

He asked this question and looked down for a moment. Abdul sat tense. He wanted the answer.

'We need a homeland, an independent Muslim state, that we build from our blood, ridding the land of our oppressors. We need to create a caliphate, where Muslims can live as Muslims without the evil influence of the Western powers. Where we can live our way and grow strong with our faith. Where Muslims will have respect and not be treated as the playthings of the Western world.

'Now let me finish on a note of hope for our people. I am in contact with kin who live in these lands. They are training soldiers and they are gathering weapons. They are creating a resistance in order to build our state. It will be hard and tiresome, but we will soon be fighting for our homeland back.'

Now there was a triumphant look on the face of the Imam. He returned to sitting quietly.

At length he finished:

'Your contact will be in touch about our next meeting.'

He tried to pull himself up. The doorman rushed over and aided him to stand. Slowly and dramatically, the doorman escorted the Imam to the door at the back of the room and they disappeared within.

With the spiritual leader gone, who had been speaking for over an hour, the room felt empty. Abdul felt like he was coming down from an emotional high, back into a reality from which the Imam had removed him for a short time.

The doorman returned and took control of the situation. The power he held over the group was not as complete as the Imam's.

'You know how this works. Two people leave quietly every fifteen minutes. I give you times, you call your cars and leave fast.'

The doorman still interested Abdul. He felt that he was trying too hard. In his black clothes with his angry-looking face, his whole facade was superficial. The more Abdul watched him the more underwhelmed he was. There was a vulnerability about him, looking so strong but hinting at an insecurity. He would show complete deference to the men in the shirts had they decided to talk back.

The wait for Abdul and Adam was not too long. They were the fourth and fifth people to leave. The same car as before waited for them outside. Abdul's head was hooded inside the car. Finally, they parked and Abdul and Adam walked to the bus station. There was some time before Abdul's coach.

He was happy that Adam sat and waited with him. It was much busier than it had been earlier that morning and the weather was still cold. The day felt older; so much had happened that it hardly felt like the same day he had arrived.

As they waited, Adam turned to Abdul:

'Thank you for coming today, Abdul. I hope it's what you were expecting.'

Abdul nodded. He was emotionally exhausted and was surprised that Adam, who had been so quiet during the day, was now talking enthusiastically.

'You sounded so committed to our cause when we spoke on the phone, but now that you have come I'm so happy.'

Abdul was satisfied to hear this. It was a rare moment for anyone to suggest they liked him. Though he wanted to, he did not reply. His day-to-day life was not conducive to making him want to speak. He was used to functional conversations: working out who would do what task in the shop and when.

Now, sat with Adam, there was a feeling deep inside him making him want to talk. When they had talked on the phone, he had spent a lot of the time listening; Adam had spoken mostly about the mosque and the Imam. He now wanted to tell Adam how much being here meant to him. Yet he didn't have the words. He felt mute.

'The Imam is a good man. He wants the best for us and Muslims. My life had been so empty, Abdul, before I met him. But he gave me something to fight for. I remember being like you, it was such a nice feeling to finally start being proud to be a Muslim.'

Abdul nodded. He searched for the words and the confidence to say them.

'Thank you, Adam, for all this.'

Adam nodded now. He turned and looked at Abdul's face and smiled. Abdul felt that Adam understood him. He was thanking him for making him feel something. It reassured Abdul to know that Adam, confident and proud, may once have been like him, lonely and quiet.

'I just wanted to say that...' his heart was beating hard, but Adam's gaze made him want to talk '... before speaking to you and meeting you and knowing people like you, I was so lonely. This is the first time... I don't know how to say it... I guess I feel like I belong...'

There was a tear in his eye as he articulated this thought. Not only had he met people he wanted to call friends, he actually faced up to how miserable his life had been beforehand.

Adam reached out and placed his hand on Abdul's shoulder.

'I know,' he said simply.

They sat quietly for a short time as a coach pulled into the bay before them. This caused the bus station's automatic doors to open and the cold air to blow in towards them. Abdul's heart sank as he saw this was his bus.

Both young men stood up. Before Abdul knew what had happened, Adam was embracing him tight.

He pulled away, looked at Abdul and said:

'Be proud to be a Muslim, and I will see you again soon.'

He turned and departed.

On the bus, Abdul found his seat. With no one next to him, he leaned against the window and rested. He felt strange, leaving. He wanted to stay; not only did he want to be away from his daily life, he wanted to be around people that made him feel proud. He did not want to be some miserable functionary struggling to keep a shop running while his mother cared for his father. He felt like there was more he could do. He had found people who would accept him. What's more, they made him feel proud to be something he had always been derided for. When he thought back to his school days, excluded for being Islamic and not white, instead of misery he now felt anger. He understood his life in a new light. He was not meant to be in this country, nor was any Muslim. He wanted to be part of building a safe place for his people. He felt he had found a purpose.

The bus reached the motorway. The world raced past Abdul as he sat thinking. His body was being returned to Milltown, but his thoughts remained in the mosque. Before his eyes closed and he slept a little, he thought of Adam as his first true friend.

Chapter Ten

Two days after turning sixteen, Darren left his grandparents' house and headed for the town centre. As he walked he pocketed the birthday money that Dawn had given him. He always felt guilty when he received such a large amount of money from his less than wealthy grandparents. He had only stayed with them briefly today as he was anxious to get into town.

Darren's actual birthday had begun fairly uneventfully, though it was later marked by his mother's changeable mood. In the morning she had not been out of bed when he awoke. Like most mornings he made himself breakfast and left a cup of tea outside her door in case she got up at a reasonable time. He then spent an hour or so watching TV and lifting weights in his room.

It was just before he went to get a second breakfast that his mother ran out of her room, spilling the tea over the floor. She was angered by the fact that she had not been up first on his birthday. She burst into Darren's day. Leaving the tea spilt outside her room, she demanded that they go out instantly. She had been saving her support allowance to treat him. So out they went, Darren in his gym clothes and his mother in her jogging bottoms and the T-shirt that she normally slept in.

In the centre of Milltown, Jane had harangued Darren into telling her where his favourite place to eat was. He didn't have one as he so rarely ate out, so they ended up in a small cafe just outside the centre. As the manic rush to get out disappeared, Jane's mood deflated. By the time they had finished eating their toast Darren could see his mother sinking into a depression. They made their way home slowly. His mother talked less as they approached their block and Darren could see that the experience had exhausted her. The only interactions they had on the way back to the flat were his mother stating 'It's nice to get out sometimes. We needed to get out for your birthday', or simply asking 'You did enjoy the breakfast, didn't you?', though she did not seem interested in the answer.

The rest of his birthday had been in the flat. Jane made a concerted effort to stay up and out of her room, despite clearly being run down and low in mood. Together they watched TV and at the end of the day Jane had gave Darren some money to buy a takeaway. It had been far from a perfect birthday, but he had appreciated it. He knew his mum did her best.

It was the care he had for his mother that had led him on today's errand. There was a bond between them that transcended a typical mother-child relationship. Darren had always felt secure with his mother. In his early years, she had defended him from his father, never letting him be hurt. She had always prioritised Darren's wellbeing and ushered him to safety.

Now he was sixteen, he wanted to provide for his mother economically. He wanted the best for her. The benefits they received were enough to survive on but they were not enough to flourish on.

There were not many options for a boy like Darren. At school, his only real success was his consistency in failure. The lower the marks he had received, the less he had cared. Even in primary school he had played truant whenever possible. He had only been good at sport.

Noting Darren's apathy for school, Frank had secured him a Saturday job in a butcher's. He had worked diligently in the butcher’s but had not taken to cutting meat. In fact, his cutting was better described as hacking. Left mainly with cleaning jobs, he felt that this was not the work for him. He needed something more active with better pay.

He found himself now outside the army recruitment shop, early on a Monday afternoon, when he should have been daydreaming in a maths lesson. Before entering, he looked at the images in the two windows. The first displayed two fully dressed soldiers, one male and one female, standing straight in commanding poses. The caption underneath read 'Do more, be more'. The most captivating aspect of this picture was the stern look on the faces of the models. Their expressions displayed strength and determination. They were not smiling, staring straight at the camera, unyielding. Why they looked so determined was unclear and left the mind to wonder. A person with no awareness of the army as an institution may have felt that picture-taking was a very serious event for these people, or that their poses took immense concentration.

There was a second picture in the window on the other side of the door. It showed the backs of four male soldiers in a very warm-looking country. The four were walking away from the camera across a dusty plain and their body language was comradely. You could see that two of the soldiers were smiling as their faces were turned in profile towards their friends. Two had their arms around each other. The caption under this image stated simply 'This is belonging'.

The army logo and the slogan 'Be the best' was present on both images.

These advertising images, like all marketing, told only a tiny and specific truth of the actual thing being marketed. For example, a fast-food restaurant, convincing the public that it only uses nationally sourced chicken, is not inclined to show images of the caged chickens being slaughtered. Likewise, the army's marketing images did not show the reality for many soldiers. The 'Do more, be more' slogan is never shown across an image of a veteran who, leaving the army mentally broken and unable to work, is sleeping rough. The 'be more' very rarely alludes to decades of suffering with PTSD after army life. The 'this is belonging' poster is unlikely to ever show the group of lads walking into the sunset with a pile of bloody enemy bodies behind them. 'Be the best' is never shown over a dead soldier's coffin.

The marketing images that Darren looked at played on the fantasies of his impressionable mind. Darren, young and innocent, was unable to see past the images in front of him. As he looked at the pictures, he imagined himself in the army uniform, strong and capable. He saw himself in heroic situations, firing his gun and earning the acclaim of his comrades. The image of belonging gripped him. With such a small family and with his diminishing group of friends, the idea of forming a close bond with other people really meant something to him. In all his imaginings, he was laughing and joking with faceless people in his head.

Having looked at these images he took a deep breath and entered the shop. Inside it felt empty. There were stacks of leaflets, more posters and a couple of desks, but very little else. He stood and waited. After a moment, two uniformed soldiers came from the back room towards Darren. From the way they were dressed, Darren could see that the younger was an officer and the older an infantry soldier. Darren noticed the contrast in their walks as they approached. The officer walked calmly and coolly towards him with a stride that suggested authority. The soldier was far more rigid. He stood much straighter and walked slightly behind the officer. The infantryman stopped still in an awkward position in the centre of the shop, standing to attention. The officer sat behind one of the desks.

Darren was a little intimidated. He didn't speak and didn't know where to look.

'Hello,' said the officer, smiling. He looked and sounded young. His face was smooth and there was no evidence that this officer could even grow a beard. His smile was quite welcoming. He leaned towards Darren in an accommodating manner.

'Are you interested in signing up or just getting a feel for the army?'

'Well...' replied Darren hesitatingly. 'I think I want to sign up.'

'Are you over sixteen?'

Darren nodded.

'Well then I think we can help,' smiled the officer. 'Perhaps we should just have a chat and then go through the forms.'

Darren smiled slightly, but he couldn't smile fully as he was so self-conscious. He didn't want to behave inappropriately or be judged badly by these people. He wanted to impress them if possible.

The officer indicated for Darren to sit on the chair opposite him. Darren awkwardly moved himself across the room towards the chair, painfully aware of his every move. He sat in an uncomfortable position right on the edge of the chair.

'So, of course, at sixteen you can't be called up, but you can enlist now.'

Darren nodded.

'You have to finish year eleven at school before you can start your training.'

Darren nodded again. He tried to nod in the most masculine way possible, with a few firm nods of the head.

'How are you doing at school?' asked the officer, raising his eyebrows.

'I'm not good,' replied Darren, lowering his head.

'That's OK,' returned the officer. He looked up at the infantryman standing at attention in the room. 'How did you do at school?' he asked him. His tone was sharp.

'I wasn't good neither, sir.' he replied without looking at him.

Darren noticed how wrinkled the standing soldier was. His face was creased, and although clearly athletic, he looked worn-out. Darren wondered briefly if any of the marks on the soldier's face were scars.

'So, it's not a problem, ' the officer stated. 'Now do you have any idea which part of the army you want to be in?'

'Not really, just the infantry really, see how it goes.'

The officer smiled again. Darren felt reassured. However, the young man's smile was actually one of relief. Much of his time was taken up displacing fantasies that people had about army life. Some wanted to go straight into the marines, others, with limited education, thought they would be flying a plane after a couple of weeks. Young people like Darren were easy, no overwhelming amount of aspiration and a malleable character.

'That's a good idea. Start off with the basics and see where you go, where you fit in. There are so many roles and specific training available. I have a leaflet here. Someone went into the infantry and came out an engineer.'

Darren was handed a leaflet. He looked over it briefly, but was too stressed to read it.

The officer again turned to the infantryman.

'Didn't you do some training in the army? Education-wise?'

'Yes sir.'

'And... what did you do?'

'Catering.'

Darren placed the leaflet down.

'What made you want to join?' the officer asked, looking at Darren again.

He hesitated at this question. He was unsure whether to be upfront about the money or offer some idealistic and patriotic explanation.

'Well, I guess I want to help the country. The money is good. I like keeping fit.'

'You have to be in good shape, but it looks like you look after yourself,' said the officer.

He went on to explain about the training, what it entailed and where it would be. He then produced a pen and a form, which he and Darren completed together.

'Now, being under eighteen, you need to get your parent or guardian to fill out this section and sign here.'

Darren's heart sank for a second. His mother didn't know he was here. However, he realised that all he needed to do was either forge his mother's signature or find her in an acquiescent mood. He could get that done.

'Finally, we've talked for a while. Do you have any questions for us? Anything at all?'

Darren sat quietly for a second. There were few questions in his head. He had been settled on enlisting for some time and felt comfortable with the decision.

Then a conversation with his grandfather echoed in his head. He remembered how his grandfather had questioned the morality of killing.

'Well, I did have one question.'

The officer nodded at him to talk.

'It's my granddad. He says that he doesn't think I would be any good at killing people. He said it's wrong.'

The officer was silent for a second, but there was no visible emotion on his face. He had heard this question many times before but had not expected it from Darren.

'Well, I think the first thing to say is that the army is not really about killing and it's a very small part of the job. Many of the modern functions of the army are not about killing or even shooting and we do a variety of other work in the world.'

Darren nodded. He already felt stupid for asking the question.

'Second, I think it is important to remember that *if* you do get in a situation where you shoot at someone, you're not shooting at innocent civilians. The people you would shoot at are not innocent. They are the enemy. They are trying to kill you and cause trouble, either here or abroad. You shoot to keep people safe, your friends and people in this country.'

This point calmed Darren a bit.

The officer turned to the soldier still standing in the same pose.

'Have you killed the enemy before?'

'Yes, sir.'

'What did you think?'

'Just have to do it, sir.'

The officer smiled again. There was something about this smile that Darren was starting to dislike.

'I think that's right. It's just what you have to do. It's not nice but it's just something that you have to do. I killed an enemy soldier once, as well...'

Had Darren been watching the standing soldier at this point he would have noticed his emotionless face display a slight disbelief.

'I killed a man with a knife, so I was very close to them. Not nice. But they were there, trying to kill my friends. It happens, and you have to react quickly.'

Darren nodded.

'Any other questions?'

Darren shook his head. Then said:

'Oh, one thing. Can I bring the form back here?'

'Of course.'

'Great.'

Darren slowly got up to leave. He had relaxed a little during the conversation, but still felt awkward.

'Well, we hope to see you again soon, Darren.'

Darren nodded and made his way towards the door. Leaving the shop, he checked the time and decided to head back to his grandparents' before returning to Milltown. He had no intention of telling Frank where he had been this afternoon, feeling it better to mention it when he actually enlisted.

He felt tired as he walked. Before going into the recruitment shop he had been stressed; now he was returning from that high. The anxiety had drained him.

The most prominent feeling in him as he walked was one of accomplishment. This was something that he had planned to do for a long time. He felt like he had taken his first firm step towards a better future. There was something about soldiering that appealed to him. The image of the soldiers, their discipline, strength and bravery. He imagined his future: himself dressed as a soldier in peak physical fitness, a group of friends around him, a sense of his own accomplishment, and his mother well looked-after.

Chapter Eleven

As Darren was making his first engagement with the British Army, Abdul was being led deeper and deeper into the Imam's ideological beliefs. He attended meetings at the extremist mosque as frequently as possible, usually once per month, and developed his relations with the members. He had managed to convince his mother that he was attending a monthly study group to maintain his education until he could take up a college place full-time. Worn-out and despondent, she had taken for granted that he was telling the truth.

When he had first entered the mosque, he had been a lonely and isolated young boy, with no direction in his life. Desperate for some mental security, he was quickly enamoured by the Imam to an extreme ideology. Abdul embraced it; the Imam gave him a sense of being part of something more, something bigger than himself.

Today, however, the conversation forced Abdul to recognise that this ideology had real-life and violent implications. The Imam had started talking about Islamic soldiers. He had explained that religious soldiers were the best soldiers as they took their strength from God. He had produced photos of Muslim soldiers in the Middle East showing their strength and ferocity. The Imam had stressed that while Muslims were not brave in the West, they could be. He stated that the West made immigrant people weak on purpose and took away their inner strength. He said that training as a Muslim soldier returned people to their true dignity as brave defenders of the religion.

This talk had moved Abdul very much. Haunted by his helplessness when his father was attacked, he felt that he had been sapped of all his inner strength by Western life. He could believe that his real destiny was to be a soldier. Had he not been raised in the West and weakened, he would have had the bravery to help his father.

The talk had moved from soldiering to terror. There was a leading question from the Imam:

'How do we become soldiers for our cause?'

There was silence in the room. Usually when the Imam raised a question he had his own answer ready. As the silence went on, the audience realised that they were expected to participate. The Imam sat quietly, patiently looking down at his crossed legs.

One of the three well-presented men in shirts was the first to speak. Of the three, Abdul judged him to be the oldest. He guessed he may be about thirty.

'We can go to the Middle East, to a training camp, and train as soldiers with our brothers.'

The Imam nodded and said nothing. The man in the shirt felt compelled to continue.

'You know, I've thought of doing it before. If we can get to, say, Turkey, and from there cross the border, we could get to a camp and learn to fight.'

The Imam nodded again; this time he replied. 'And if it is so easy to get on a plane and get to a training camp, why have you not already done it?'

Now there was an embarrassed silence.

He replied with much more humility, not making eye contact with the Imam, 'I guess I don't know where to go.'

'Our brothers training for the cause do not readily advertise their location to the enemy. They must remain secret,' stated the Imam. 'There is no easy way to find them. You would need *someone* to get you in the right direction, and even then it would not be guaranteed you would find them. How else can we become soldiers?'

The question was posed to the room. The Imam had a satisfied look on his face. He seemed to be taking some pleasure from challenging his flock.

The second of the men in the shirts now answered. He was also well presented, with an expensive shirt and fresh haircut. As he spoke Abdul noticed he had a strange mannerism with his arm. He would lift it every few sentences and shake it slightly, uncovering a large watch that rested under his sleeve. He would then pull his sleeve again over the watch before shaking his sleeve again a few sentences later.

'I think we can do things here in the UK to support our brothers abroad...' he said, pulling his sleeve back over his watch. 'We can help our brothers by launching attacks against the people here.'

'What do you mean?' asked the Imam in a soft tone.

The younger one turned to the older man in the shirt. It was clear that this was a discussion they had had before.

'I mean plan attacks here in the UK. Say, attack people in the streets. I think it will drain security resources and make people fear attacking us abroad, because they will be scared about vengeance on their doorstep.'

The Imam sat forward slightly and looked at the speaker. 'You mean attacking innocent people? Will that not make them want to attack us more?'

The young man in the shirt was taken aback by the direct contradiction from the Imam. When he had first spoken he had been confident. Now he slumped down.

'This is the point,' continued the Imam to the room in general. 'We need to defend ourselves, but does that mean attacking undefended, unaware people?'

This time the two who had already spoken answered simultaneously. The elder said firmly 'No' while the younger shyly stated 'Yes'. The two looked at each other. There was a look of disgust on the face of the younger, so much so that it implied he would make the older a victim of the terror he planned.

The Imam laughed. The first time Abdul had ever heard him laugh.

'Well, we must maintain order. So, I would like you to explain yourselves fully, but one at a time.'

The Imam was thoroughly engaged in this contest. He slowly and regally raised his hand to the older man to explain himself first.

The elder spoke, addressing himself mainly to the younger. As he spoke, he inclined his head in an unaggressive but assertive manner.

'We shouldn't, no, *can't*, attack innocent people. We must only defend our homeland when it is invaded. I think I have two reasons for this. One is that we must not make ourselves look like animals before our enemies. We should be magnanimous and show that we have a moral and peaceful high ground against their decadence. If we go killing innocents, we give their governments the justification to paint us as evil and attack us in our lands again. No matter how angry we are, we must be disciplined enough to only attack those that are directly attacking us. Second, where in the scripture does it say that it is OK to kill innocents? It doesn't. Only that we must defend ourselves when attacked.'

He took a deep breath and sat back. A perceptive eye would have noticed his hand shaking slightly from adrenaline.

The Imam slowly raised his hand towards the other to allow him to speak.

Before the younger started speaking, Abdul noticed a look on his face. He appeared twisted to Abdul's eyes.

'I don't want to kill innocent people. But they are not innocent. They know what their governments do, going to our homeland and killing our people. And they still elect them, they are so ignorant to our suffering, and that makes them part of it. So, I have two points. Just because someone does not shoot a gun does not mean they are not part of the Western oppression. The second point, like I said before, if we cannot go to help the fight directly, we must help it here. We must attack people here.'

Abdul's reaction to this viewpoint was abhorrence. He could see himself as a soldier abroad, fighting for the cause. However, the idea of going and attacking random and undefended people did not seem honourable to him. When he imagined himself doing it his stomach turned.

The Imam interjected as Abdul sat troubled with his conscience:

'These are two interesting viewpoints. I notice the rest of you will not talk, but it is OK as we are short of time. Before you come here again I must ask that you all go and think. Think about what you can and will do for our brothers abroad and we can build on this next time. The only advice I will give is that you must let yourself be guided by God. Some people will be capable of things others are not. I want you all to listen to what you feel God wants you to do.'

With that he struggled up. The doorman jumped to his aid and supported him through to the back room. The Imam stopped at the door and turned back to the crowd. He summoned Adam forward and the three went through.

Abdul was too perplexed by his own conscience to wonder what Adam had been summoned for. He thought about what he could and should do. He did not want to commit acts of terror in this country; he imagined training abroad. But how would he get there, and could he abandon his mother?

Adam returned from the room with the doorman and the group slowly left the mosque. There were two individuals Abdul noticed leaving before him. One was the young man in the shirt. His body language displayed annoyance. He walked slightly in front of the older man to the door and was clearly angered by their discussion. Second, Abdul noticed an older scruffily dressed member of the group who had been a new attendee just before him. He was usually a shy and unhappy-looking man; however, as he left, there was something different about his demeanour. He seemed happy with himself and much more relaxed than usual. He even smiled at the large doorman as he left.

Abdul did not think much of it and he continued to mull over whether he had the strength to fight for his cause. Was his disinclination to commit terror a form of weakness? Before he knew it, he was at the bus station with Adam, waiting for his coach to Milltown. Adam was quiet and thoughtful as they sat there.

Abdul spoke first, becoming curious about Adam and the Imam. 'You don't have to tell me, but what did you do in the Imam's private room?'

Adam smiled. He turned to look at Abdul and said, 'I visit the Imam quite often and I think he trusts me. It has taken a long time. I will tell you, but not yet.'

Abdul was satisfied with this. His mind then returned to the discussion from earlier.

'The discussion today was difficult.'

Adam turned to Abdul again.

'It is something I think about a lot. What can I do, and what should I do? I want to do something, but I don't know what.'

'I feel the same,' replied Abdul, glad to hear that he was not the only one unclear about what to do. 'Can I be honest, Adam? I didn't like what the young guy in the shirt was saying.'

'Me neither,' Adam said, looking away from Abdul. 'I understand his arguments, but I think we need to be clever about what we do. He's too bloodthirsty and unforgiving.'

Abdul nodded, relieved to hear that Adam had the same reservations.

Adam continued. 'I think I know what I'll do. I'll speak with you before I do it, as I would like you with me.'

Abdul smiled. These words made him feel proud. He had only known Adam for a short time but felt an immense trust and care for him.

'Good,' he said simply.

The coach arrived and, after being embraced by Adam, he got aboard. He thought about Adam's plans and whether the angry young man actually had the drive to make good on his threats. Before getting back to Milltown he resolved that he would support Adam in any way he could. He had never felt a connection to anyone the way he did to Adam. He did not want to lose him.

Chapter Twelve

After this last conversation, Abdul was resolved to leave Milltown if this was what Adam had in mind. He did not know when or how this would happen, but he did not expect it to occur as suddenly as it did.

Late one evening Abdul was sitting in his room. His mother was closing the shop while his father sat silently in the living room in front of a loud television. Without even being in the room, Abdul could see his empty face staring at the screen. Abdul was thinking about sleeping but his mind was elsewhere. He was in a restless mood.

Then his phone rang.

There was an unknown number on the screen. He guessed this may be Adam, he so frequently changed his number. He answered the phone but was not even able to finish the word 'hello'. Adam's voice interrupted him:

'Abdul, something awful happened.'

'What?'

'I was going to see the Imam today. The block was surrounded by police. I think they've taken him. Someone's grassed. I'm worried they will come for us.'

Abdul froze. Fear gripped him and his breathing became shorter. He opened his mouth to talk but no words came out. Instead, he sat on his bed, holding his phone to his ear firmly, a slight tremor in his body.

'I don't have time to go into details, and I need to hurry. I have a plan.'

'OK...' breathed Abdul.

'The Imam gave me details of people in France who can get me to the Middle East. They can get me to a training camp.'

In the space of a few sentences, Abdul had found that the mosque was gone and now Adam may be leaving as well. His fear about the police coming for him was overshadowed by a fear of Adam leaving.

'Here's the thing, though, Abdul. I don't know why, but I trust you. I know that it wasn't you that grassed. At first, I trusted no one that had been there, but I want to trust you. I want you to come with me. I've booked two tickets for a ferry leaving tomorrow. You need to get a coach leaving Milltown at midnight, and I will meet you in London. Then we will travel to Dover. Are you coming?'

Abdul hesitated, trying to take all this in.

He thought of his stressed mother, his redundant father, his mundane existence and lack of meaningful relations with anybody in the town. His answer was there:

'I will come, Adam.'

'Good. The bus leaves at midnight. Pack light. Take your passport. We have to go fast. When you arrive in London, call this number and I'll find you.'

He hung up. Abdul was alone in his room. He checked the time. Ten. Milltown bus station was not far. He knew he could easily get there by midnight. The tricky thing was leaving the flat unnoticed.

Quickly he packed his bag, taking his unused passport from the drawer. It was still in date. He had applied for the passport before his father was attacked. At that time, he had thought he may need proof of identity at college.

Before leaving his room, he deleted his internet history and switched off his laptop. He slipped on his battered trainers. Finally, he placed a pillow under the duvet of his bed to make it look like he was sleeping.

Outside his room he was lucky. His father was sleeping in front of the television. The noise from the TV set was enough to mask the sound of him leaving. He looked at his father asleep on the sofa. He felt both sympathy and regret for this ruined man. He had had so many plans, all trashed by the violence of the robbers. He regretted that he did not know his father, not really. All his life there had been a distance. Since the attack, there had been no prospect of bridging that gap.

Passing through the front door of the flat, he descended the stairs. At the bottom, his luck ran out. His mother was coming up to the flat. She looked pale and exhausted.

'Where are you going, Abdul, at this time?' she asked.

Abdul froze for a second but managed to answer: 'To see Ibrahim. He's out of bread and asked if I would take him some up.'

'OK,' replied the despondent Awet. 'Be quiet when you come back in.'

'I will.'

They passed each other. As he had felt sympathy for his father, he felt a shattering sorrow for leaving his mother. Life was grinding her down. All she did was work and care for her husband. Now her life would be even harder.

He could justify leaving. Exiting the house, he reminded himself of what the Imam had said, that being in this country was poisonous for Muslims. That they needed to build a safe homeland for all Muslims away from the pain of this country. By leaving, he told himself, he was going to fight to make life better for more people.

Despite rationalising his guilt about leaving, he still loved her. In his life he felt that two people had shown him real care and concern: his mother and now Adam.

He went out into the night. His last night in Milltown. It was ten past ten now; he had plenty of time. A thought occurred to him as he was standing in the empty street. To go and see Ibrahim. He didn't know why he felt the need to do this, but he decided to go regardless.

Abdul took off at a fast pace.

Stomping through the deserted backstreets of Milltown, Abdul felt alone. He passed through the shadowy, desolate town towards his brother's flat. He liked it like this; he could go unnoticed. Too many times on these streets had he been looked at funny, even insulted. As he passed certain spaces, he thought back to these incidents. He was at peace knowing that soon he would be leaving forever.

Arriving at Ibrahim's flat he buzzed his way up. Ibrahim, on the receiver, was surprised to hear Abdul so late but admitted him to the flat. Abdul ascended the stairs towards his brother's door. The flat was dark. It seemed that a dull smoke lingered in the air in the flat, taking the edge off the light that shone from the bulb.

'I didn't expect you so late,' said Ibrahim. He appeared pale, as Abdul was accustomed to see him look. 'I should have been working, really, but I changed my shift.'

Abdul was quiet. He entered the flat and sat in the living room lit by a lamp in the corner. Abdul had to clear a space for himself on the sofa before sitting down. Ibrahim entered the room behind him, coughing a little.

'Do you want a drink or something, little brother?'

Abdul resented Ibrahim's use of the term 'little'. He was slightly taller than Ibrahim now and the only thing smaller about Abdul was his age. He knew he was certainly not smaller in intellect.

'I don't have long, Ibrahim. Sit down, I need to tell you something.'

Ibrahim, who had clearly been sleeping before Abdul arrived, collapsed opposite Abdul on an armchair. His eyes started to close and he was longing for his bed. He sat on a pile of washing that had been there for weeks. He looked curious at Abdul's statement, but was still not quite engaged.

Abdul, until he heard the words come out of his own mouth, did not know what he was about to say. Words just poured from him.

'I'm leaving. I know it's a shock, but a friend of mine is going abroad and I'm going with them.'

Abdul knew it was a risk speaking to Ibrahim, but something was compelling him to be honest.

This comment shook Ibrahim a little more awake.

'What do you mean, bro? Where you going?'

'Just a friend I met at the mosque...' Abdul was looking anywhere but directly at Ibrahim. 'Listen, my friend is going to go and fight in the Middle East, and I want to go with him... There isn't anything for us here.'

If Ibrahim had just exercised a little more self-control, he would not have reacted the way he did. He would have gone along with what Abdul said to find more information, then discreetly passed it to an authority. Understandably, Ibrahim did not react like this.

'What do you mean, going to the Middle East? Are you mental, bro?'

He sat up, edged forward, looking at his younger brother. Abdul could feel Ibrahim's anguish radiating across the room at him. He wouldn't be deterred by Ibrahim, for whom, of late, he had felt a slight contempt.

'Ibrahim, don't be angry, it's more complicated than that. I've been going to this mosque, the Imam explained it all, Ibrahim.'

'Explained what...?'

'That we shouldn't be here, that this society is poison for us. We need a homeland and I want to go and fight for it. The Imam said that we were forced to come here because of what they did to us in history.'

Ibrahim, wide-eyed, watched his brother talking.

'That's mental, Abdul, just mental. I bet Mum doesn't know where you're going.'

Ibrahim repeated the word 'mental'. In his state of shock he could not find another word.

'No. And it's not mental. Look, Ibrahim, look at you and this life. The Imam said they make us live like this to stop us being true Muslims. We can be better than this, Ibrahim. We can live good and better lives...'

'Shut up, Abdul. I always thought you were the smart one. You sound like a fucking idiot. Every sentence you say starts with “the Imam says”, like you've been brainwashed.'

Ibrahim was standing now. This was the most irate that Abdul had ever seen him. He paced around the room and moved his hands erratically as he spoke.

'You think that this Imam gives a shit about you? Fuck me, Abdul! You think he cares about Muslims and you living a good life? You think anyone cares? We are just poor fucking people...'

He had been heading towards the door but now he turned. He looked directly at Abdul. He addressed him in a quieter and more deliberate tone now. He had found what he wanted to say.

'Look, Abdul. Life is hard, bro. It's awful sometimes. You get born into some random family who make choices for you and then some of us get fucked up. Like us. We were happy, then Dad moved us to Milltown, I made bad friends and you have to work in a shop instead of going to school...'

Abdul sat quietly looking at the floor.

'I know it's shit. But this is the point, Abdul. Because we don't have anything, people want to use us. Like me. I have this shit job with this wanker manager who makes me work extra hours, and I just have to fucking do it to pay the rent and buy food. I was shit at school, I messed around, and now here I am. He doesn't care, he just wants to make me work.'

Abdul still sat looking at the floor. Ibrahim felt that he was listening to him. He felt strange, speaking like this. He had never spoken about his life with his brother before. Now though, he felt compelled to.

'It's worse for you, Abdul. You were so clever and then that attack happens and you're stuck looking after that father of ours who brought us here and fucked it up. I know why you want to get away. But this Imam, he's like my manager, Abdul. He is. He doesn't care about you, or how you live. Not really. He just wants to use you. He has filled your head with bullshit to get you to go to the Middle East and fight for them, but they don't give a fuck. They just want another little Muslim boy willing to die because they love the power. At least my manager doesn't make me die. These people just want power. They get off on it. They tell you anything to get you to do stuff.'

Abdul still sat quietly. Ibrahim had amazed himself this evening. He had never spoken so fully about how much he hated his life. He tried one more point.

'For my part, Abdul, I'm sorry. I work and sleep and I just left you to it at home. I'm really sorry. I should have done more. I should have checked you were OK, but I didn't. I just left you to it. I'm really sorry.'

Abdul did not answer straight away. While Ibrahim stared at him across the dark room he stayed sitting looking at the floor. He was moved by what Ibrahim had said, and Ibrahim could see this. Barely breathing, he hoped that he had got through to his younger brother.

'The thing is, Ibrahim...' Abdul began slowly, clearly thinking about what he would say. 'You have never been there. You have never heard the Imam speak.' Abdul looked up now straight at Ibrahim. 'How can you judge what the Imam thinks about me if you have never even seen him. You have never experienced God or being a Muslim like I have. This isn't bad, Ibrahim. It's good. It's actually amazing. To be around people who understand what Islam is...'

Abdul looked enthusiastic and engaged, emotions that Ibrahim had not seen him display since childhood.

'I don't feel like you understand, Ibrahim. I want you to come with me. Away from this life you're living. The Imam used to say that life is so much richer as a Muslim with something to fight for.'

'Can you hear yourself, Abdul?' Ibrahim was exacerbated. What more could he say? Now anger was his primary emotion. He took a step towards his brother, then turned towards the door.

'Where are you going?'

'Just stay here.'

'Where are you going, Ibrahim?' Abdul was more assertive with his second question.

'To make a call. Just stay here.'

'Who are you calling?'

Ibrahim didn't answer. He continued to walk towards the door.

In a moment, all the possibilities of who Ibrahim may be calling raced through Abdul's head. The police, his mother, a friend? All would be detrimental to his plans. Ibrahim was at the door. His phone was in his hand.

The tragedy of Abdul's next act was that it was facilitated by Ibrahim's cluttered lifestyle. If he had been a little tidier, if he had not lived in such squalor, Abdul would not have had a weapon so close to hand. Ibrahim did live in squalor. Two nights ago, he had been eating beans from a saucepan. Instead of washing it he had left the pan on the floor next to where Abdul was now sitting. Two nights ago, when Ibrahim had placed this pan down after having eaten, he did not even have the nucleus of an idea that this pan may be used in an act of aggression. Tonight, Abdul noticed the pan. He acted on impulse.

Before his conscious mind could comprehend what he was doing, he clutched the pan. Next, he was on his feet, looking at Ibrahim, who, with his back turned, had just passed into the hall. Abdul took three fast strides, the pan raised above his head.

Down it crashed onto the back of Ibrahim's head. Wielded with a force Abdul had never used before. Ibrahim fell to his knees. Again, Abdul struck him. A cold, hard blow to the back of the head. The pan made a dull thud as it connected with the skull of his brother. A final blow he delivered to Ibrahim.

Blood poured from his head, soaking into the grey carpet. He lay motionless on the floor. Abdul's grip on the pan began to loosen. He stepped back from the blood. A strange mix of feelings filled his spinning mind. His stomach turned in disgust. This was countered by a feeling of vindication. He felt he had defended himself and Adam from a Western and fake Muslim. He almost smiled. He had shown the necessary strength and conviction.

He took a deep breath and steadied himself. Calmly he picked up his bag and his coat. He looked around the flat. He noticed some ten-pound notes on a shelf in the hallway and placed them in his pocket. He left the flat without looking again at his brother.

On his way down, his thoughts turned towards the neighbours below: would they have heard the argument between the brothers? On leaving the flat he looked towards their windows. They were dark, the flat showed no sign of life. Perhaps they were used to noise from Ibrahim's abode, perhaps they were not in.

For the last time, he stepped out into the dark Milltown night. He checked the time and set off towards the bus station. His brother lay, bleeding, alone and quiet on the floor in his flat. Abdul would never know if he would get up again.

If anyone who had known Abdul as a young boy, his teachers at school or his peers in his family mosque, could see him now they would not recognise him. The caring and empathetic young boy, who was so quiet and rarely resorted to violence, was gone. They would be shocked to see him walking away from his brother, lying wounded, hardly seeming to care. Perhaps they would ask themselves what could have gone so wrong? How could one of the nicest young boys they had had in their class, in their mosque, at their home to play, act so callously? Would they reflect on the damage that can be caused to a tender soul by a vile environment?

By the time his mother awoke at five in the morning, Abdul was close to London. By the time she was frustrated that Abdul was not up and helping in the shop, he was embracing Adam and planning their journey to the ferry. It was eight-thirty before Awet looked into Abdul's room to drag him out of bed. As she realised he was not there, he was already on his way to Dover.

Awet's surprise that Abdul was not in his bed led her to call both Abdul and Ibrahim. Abdul no longer had his phone; Ibrahim was unable to answer. It was past midday before

Awet, overcome with worry, closed the shop and walked to Ibrahim's flat. Abdul would never see the horror on her face as she saw her eldest son lying in his own blood on the hallway floor.

As Awet looked on in tears, unable to piece together how this could have happened, Abdul and Adam were on a ferry to France. Though he sometimes felt twinges of guilt or worry about the attack, he felt mainly at peace. He never wanted to be in Milltown again, he never wanted to experience that life again. Both young men felt they were following their destiny, to be true Muslims and fight for a true cause.

Chapter Thirteen

Darren walked out of the barracks in his civilian clothes. He was just over seventeen now, growing into a man. He was heading for the train station to make his way back to Milltown. He was accompanied by Shane, a soldier in his brigade. Shane was an interesting character and Darren had not made up his mind about him. When on his own, he liked him very much. He was quiet and sensible and the two found a lot of common interests, especially boxing. However, in a group of more than four people, Shane underwent a metamorphosis, becoming the group clown. There had been countless times when, unable to keep his mouth shut, he had caused the whole brigade to undergo punishments. He became hyperactive when he had an audience, desiring constant attention.

Today, it was just the two of them heading to the nearby station. Shane was going to see his father, who had also been in the military. Shane, from a young age, had never imagined doing anything else. The family was a military family, always serving in the infantry. His older brother, also a soldier, had risen quickly through the ranks. Darren couldn't imagine Shane doing the same. He lacked the discipline and refinement to make an officer.

The two of them walked at a reasonable pace, carrying rucksacks. A passer-by would guess they were soldiers. Since undergoing training the young men had started to walk in a military fashion, tall and always marching. They were smart as well. Darren's shirt was ironed and he no longer threw on the first clothes he noticed when getting up.

The two of them chatted idly. They reflected on training and whether they would see any action in their military careers. Shane hoped they would. He told Darren that his father, a Falklands veteran, said it created a bond between the soldiers that he had never experienced again. The reliance they had on each other out there, wherever they may be posted, would be something else.

Darren reflected quietly on this. He was proud to be in the army. The reminders from the officers of what they were doing and what they trained for made him proud. The idea of looking out for each other while protecting the country reinforced the image of the army he had had before enlisting. To put his training to use, he thought, would be honourable.

However, whenever he thought about leaving the UK, there were two nagging doubts in his head. The first was his mother. He didn't know how she would cope with the worry of him being abroad. He knew she would struggle without him coming home often. The second worry was his grandfather. He would have an opinion and Darren was not sure he wanted to hear it. Since joining the army, a distance had already grown between them, and this sat uneasily with him.

At the station, Shane's train arrived quickly and the two men embraced; not a feminine embrace but a firm masculine one, befitting soldiers. Shane's hand landed heavily on Darren's shoulder. Darren felt his firmness. They wished each other good leave and said when they would be back.

This gave Darren some rare time alone with his thoughts. As a soldier, he felt that every second of his day was organised. He sometimes had free time at barracks, but was always surrounded by people. There was a tight bond with his comrades; they were like a second family. He always thought about his mother, though.

Jane had become a worry for Darren since enlisting. He spoke to her as often as possible, but there was a distance. He did not know what she did with herself when he was not there and knew that she rarely left the flat. She had actually mentioned going to church a couple of times, but Darren thought little of this. He was glad she was going out a bit.

He was sending her money often. She was sometimes reluctant to take it, but always did. This made him feel proud, to think he was now giving her something back.

He waited for the train. A cool breeze blew and he looked into the sky. It was dark, though it was already mid-morning. Clouds were covering the sky. Eventually the train arrived.

*

A few weeks after leaving Milltown, Abdul had formed a close bond with his comrade Adam. The journey had pushed them firmly together. The outside world changed daily, but Adam was a constant.

Leaving the UK had been stressful. Abdul hardly slept on the bus but was elated to meet Adam. The past seemed to evaporate when he met him. He was no longer Abdul, the timid Milltown boy, victim of bullying, the shop worker; he was a soldier. They were on a crusade.

Crossing the English Channel had gone well, but the two of them were lost trying to get to Paris. Eventually they had navigated the French train system and ended up in the Gare du Nord. Adam had an address to find in Paris, given to him by the Imam. But they had no way of getting their bearings in the daunting city and both were reluctant to ask strangers. Eventually, Adam had decided to lift a map. After selecting and discreetly taking a street-atlas they had inspected it on some steps near the Gare de L'Est. They found the street and three hours later they arrived outside the property. This followed a lot of wrong turns.

When Abdul looked back, he felt that entering the address in Paris was a pivotal moment for them. They stepped out of the city and into the protection of the terrorist cell. Abdul felt his entire world was reconfigured at this point. The building was organised by four large and toughened men. The name of the Imam had been known to the men and, communicating in broken English, they had taken them in. Together, Abdul and Adam were kept with four French recruits in a large upstairs room. They handed over their passports to the men. The treatment was cold and they were largely ignored. Abdul had appeared uncomfortable and worried. Adam, comforting Abdul, had explained that this treatment was necessary as they had to earn trust. The stronger they were, the more respect they would earn. Adam promised that he would earn trust for the two of them, and had promptly tried to ingratiate himself with the four organisers.

From Paris, after a few days, they had been bundled into a minibus. Six recruits, travelling with three men. The transporting men had established a fear in the recruits. They kept their passports and made known the knives and guns that they had stowed on the bus. Adam, Abdul, and their new French comrades were quiet as they travelled. Adam and Abdul struggled to speak to the other recruits due to the language barrier, but there was an unspoken understanding between them.

An uncomfortable journey followed. They spent three days travelling through various countries before arriving in Greece. Here, meeting with two further recruits, they had stayed for just over a week, hidden in an old farmhouse which seemed to be in the middle of nowhere. One night, they had been taken to the sea and put on a boat waiting at a small harbour. This had been the scariest part of the journey for Abdul. Aside from the ferry from the UK, he had never been on the sea, and never on such a dubious-looking boat. They did make it to Turkey and were driven to their current location.

Throughout the journey, Adam had been resolute. He had not once wavered, hardly appearing bothered by their situation. Inspired by Adam, Abdul had become calmer. He had such faith in Adam and knew he would see him through. He looked up to him, he trusted him and he was unconditionally obedient. He had given himself to him and Adam was aware of this. The dynamic between the two had developed, Adam taking the role of leader, Abdul following. The two fulfilled their roles in this relationship: Adam could act knowledgeable, following the example of the Imam, to recruit and lead people in the cause. Abdul felt a reflected strength from Adam's determination. He felt a dedication to him which emboldened them both.

They understood they would next be taken into Syria and then to a training camp. They were told that this final border crossing was the last dangerous one, but they had to wait until nightfall. A certain border crossing station had been partially bribed, but they had to wait until the correct staff were on shift in order to cross.

It was early evening now. Abdul and Adam were sitting together next to the stone wall. Abdul had stolen some glances at the land around them through a partly open window. It was dry and warm, a heat he had never felt before. The landscape was foreign to him and he felt far removed from the rainy post-industrial town in which he had been brought up. Milltown, and the events of his life there, felt like someone else's life. He sat quietly. By the door of the room a gunman was sitting.

Adam turned to Abdul:

'How are you doing? You managed to sleep?'

Abdul shook his head. Adam continued in a low voice:

'You need to sleep when you can. You learn this.'

Abdul nodded.

'I discovered this when I was sleeping outside. Wherever there is a quiet spot, you take one, two hours if you can get it. We should try and do the same now.'

Abdul was tired. He couldn't remember his last good sleep. He leaned his head against the wall and closed his eyes. He wanted sleep.

Then a question rose in his head.

'I never knew you had been homeless, Adam,' he said. He realised he knew very little about Adam's background. He gave a lot of advice, but very little detail of where it came from.

'Hm,' replied Adam, 'I was young.'

Abdul didn't push it. He never did. Independently, Adam continued the conversation. Inside, Abdul was elated; he felt like he was being drawn deeper into Adam's confidence.

'I never really talk about it, but my father kicked me out. I was a lot of trouble then, and he was sick of me. He was a fake Muslim anyway. Always drinking, never praying...'

Adam pulled a face as he spoke about his father.

'Anyway, I got kicked out, about eighteen years old. I went to the council and they said it was my fault I was homeless and didn't put me anywhere. I ended up sleeping outside.'

Adam was talking quietly and slowly. Abdul couldn't tell if he was ashamed or whether it was just difficult for him to recount.

'It was then that I met the Imam. He was preaching at another mosque then. He sorted a room for me to rent and started to teach me about life. He was a good man, Abdul. I wish you could have known him longer.'

Abdul nodded. He wished this too.

'He helped a lot of young men, Abdul. He was charitable and he was good. He had the kindest heart.'

Abdul nodded again. He was happy to be hearing Adam's thoughts. Since they had left, Adam had interrogated him about every aspect of his life. The only thing that Adam didn't know about, that Abdul would not say out loud, was the attack on his brother. This was something he did not want to put into words. Most of the time, the memory was out of his mind.

'I think you're doing well, Abdul. You never slept out before, always had a bed to sleep on, you're doing OK with the travel. It will get worse, I think. So try and sleep now.'

Abdul listened and leaned back again on the wall. His last thoughts as he slipped into a light sleep were of Adam. He felt devoted to him.

Chapter Fourteen

After nearly two years in the army, Darren was beginning to feel like a stranger in Milltown. He was now over eighteen and felt more at home in the barracks than with his mother.

While Darren could now support Jane economically, there was no denying that their relationship had altered. When he came back, it took longer each time for them to start acting like a mother and son again. When it finally started to feel like it had in the old days, it was time to return to barracks. The experience had taught Darren how relationships need time. This was especially true for Jane. He felt every time he returned, he needed to win her trust. She didn't seem to want to get comfy with him around again knowing he would disappear. Darren had underestimated how much his mother needed him around.

Darren had changed physically since being in the army. On leave today, now in his old flat, he was tall and thickset. Where the sleeves on his T-shirts had once been baggy, his large arms now filled the space, making them cling tightly to his body. Anyone could see that he was in peak physical condition. He enjoyed looking at his muscles in the mirror, indulging his vanity. Yet while he had grown in stature, he was still Darren: still caring and thoughtful, seeking positive interactions with his mother.

On returning to his old home yesterday he had been met with a bit of a shock. He had returned with news that he was anxious to tell his mother. He had hoped to tell her last night when he had arrived but had first been taken aback by her news: she was seeing someone, a new man. Having heard what his mother had to say, he had gone straight to bed.

This morning, as usual, he had woken first, thinking to make her a drink and leave it outside her door. After leaving his room he headed towards the kitchen, still dwelling on what Jane had told him. He heard movement in the kitchen as he approached and wondered if his mother was up already. As he reached the door and looked inside he froze. A man was standing in his kitchen. He was reaching for cups from the cupboard and had put the kettle on. He appeared roughly his mother's age, well presented, smart-looking.

Darren was aghast. He guessed who this was, but why was he here? It was the man his mother had told him about yesterday. In her words this was 'a male friend who she was getting close with'. Now he was here, making tea. How had he let himself in? Did he have a key already?

Darren continued to weigh him up. He noticed the man was wearing a neat buttoned shirt and dark trousers, like jeans. It struck him that this gentleman was much shorter than himself.

It was the stranger, or intruder, as Darren labelled him, who broke the silence first. Darren was too startled to act.

'You must be Darren,' said the stranger. He beamed at Darren. 'I'm Mark.' There was no malice, nothing unfriendly about this man at all, much to Darren's disappointment. The only dislikeable thing about him was that his accent was slightly posher than Darren's.

Darren just nodded in answer.

'Sorry if I woke you, I try to be here sometimes when your mother wakes up.'

'Right...'

'Shall I make you a drink?'

'I'll make my own.'

'Of course.'

Without any sign of disappointment or annoyance he stepped aside to allow Darren to make himself a drink. Despite there being a mug out for him, Darren selected another from the cupboard. To his irritation, the stranger continued to talk to him.

'Your mother tells me you're in the army,' said Mark as Darren poured water into his cup.

Darren grunted in the affirmative. He aggressively squeezed the tea bag and stirred in the sugar. The milk was already out on the side.

'She said you've been there about two years now?'

'About that, yeah.'

Having made his drink, Darren had nothing to focus his attention on. He felt trapped in the conversation. He had to turn around and engage with the stranger opposite him. He looked down at the tea he was cradling.

'So,' continued his mother's new man, leaning on the counter opposite Darren. 'Do you enjoy the army?'

'Yeah, I guess.'

'Is there a lot of training? What about the discipline side of things?'

'Yeah...' Darren didn't want to talk. He had never had a stranger in this space before; he didn't like it. He wanted this interaction over with and for this man to leave so he could spend some time with his mother.

'Are you learning a lot in the army? I hear you can learn other skills. Mechanics and that kind of thing.'

'You can, but I haven't done that yet.' This was certainly something that Darren didn't want to talk about. He had expected by now to have begun some kind of course.

There was an awkward silence. Mark seemed to be running out of questions.

'Your mother speaks very highly of you, you know. When I first met her, you were all she talked about.'

'Hmm,' grunted Darren again. 'How long you staying today?' This was the first question posed by him. He looked into his cup as he asked it.

'Well, I spoke to Jane and I think she wanted us all to go for a drink today. I know a really nice cafe just outside of town.'

'Yeah,' said Darren despondently. He was still not looking directly at Mark.

Suddenly he necked his tea fast. It was still hot and scolded his throat as he drank it. He tried to show no discomfort.

'I just realised I said I would visit my grandparents today. Maybe I'll see you later.'

The stranger, who had looked so positive, despite all of Darren's rebuttals, finally looked a little downcast.

'Of course,' he said.

Darren left the kitchen, put on his jacket and shoes and left the flat. He realised he had not brushed his teeth but couldn't face going back. He checked the change in his pocket as he descended the staircase. There was enough for the bus. He felt relieved as he left. Since hearing about this man, he had felt awful, and meeting him had not helped. He couldn't help feeling like his mother had replaced him. He also felt guilty as he knew his behaviour towards Mark would upset Jane. His overriding emotion was one of loss. He felt that a space that belonged to him and his mum was gone.

At the bus stop, he had to wait twenty minutes. Luckily, the weather was not cold although it was slightly cloudy. The background noise of the busy road drifted out of focus as he started to reflect. He did enjoy life as a soldier, he told himself. He wanted to be a man and be respected for his role. But experiences like this morning played on his mind.

Of course, he enjoyed the training and the feeling of duty. He was told, and really felt, that he was representing more than himself when in the uniform. There was a sense of pride that he was part of the institution charged with defending civilians. There were some elements of the training he had found hard, some exercises which had been quite humiliating and pointless. For instance, his platoon had once been ordered to carry stones from one side of a field to the other. They were then ordered to carry them back. As he became more tired with the stones in the heat he wanted to storm away from the barracks. He understood that this was an exercise in developing discipline, which his officer had said was crucial in battle. Overall, he felt he had proved himself and that his experience was broadly positive.

That was not to say that leaving home and staying in barracks had been without its challenges. It had been hard to make friends with the other soldiers; being surrounded by new people he had realised how much he cared for his mother's company. He had also become annoyed by the feeling that he was being overlooked to learn other skills. He wanted to learn mechanics or engineering, but no opportunity had yet been offered.

Discovering that his mother had become so close with a new man set doubts in his mind. She was clearly looking for company and Darren felt cut out. While he could help her buy things he wondered if it would be better if he were around more. In the coming months that would be an impossibility.

As the bus arrived, these doubts continued swirling around Darren's head. He sat quietly next to the window on the bus gazing absently as the world moved past him.

Arriving in his grandparents' town, where he had been born, he began looking forward to seeing Frank and Dawn. The Milltown bus arrived in the centre of the town. Darren decided to make the twenty-minute walk to his grandparents rather than wait for another bus.

The journey took him away from the high street, along the main road. Slowly, the numbers of shops and pubs were replaced by terraces and blocks of flats and even some parks. The town itself had hardly changed since the night Darren and his mother had fled to Milltown. There was the odd new development interspersed between the older buildings of the town, but nothing had changed drastically.

Roughly halfway to his grandparents' house, Darren became aware of a pub on the other side of the main road. There was a moderate amount of traffic passing on the single carriageway, so he was surprised that this pub had caught his eye. He slowed down to look at the building.

He had noticed movement inside the pub. The sound of the locks were heard being aggressively opened. Out, in a hurry, came a short man followed by a thin woman of a similar age. Both looked worn-out by life. Darren noticed the man was unshaven, his skin was aged and he had bags under his eyes. It surprised him to see this exhausted-looking couple moving so quickly. Darren noticed their clothes looked shabby and in need of a wash.

Outside the pub the man seemed to rally. Despite the small woman trying to drag him away, he turned back to yell at the open door.

'Fucking thieves, we're not coming to this shithole again!'

Darren noticed a third dark figure in the doorway of the pub take a step towards the outside. At this, the aggression of the rallying man dissipated and he visibly baulked, pulling himself away from the pub. The figure inside the pub, who Darren could only just make out in the dark doorway, shook his head before slamming the door.

The dejected couple gathered themselves. The man was first to move away, pulling his jacket around him. He looked at the woman with her messy hair and embarrassed look on her face. The man lost patience with her, with this situation and apparently with life in general. He threw his hands up at her, gesturing aggressively that they should leave. They turned.

At this moment the man looked over the road and noticed Darren standing and watching.

'You got a fucking problem, bastard?' yelled the man from the other side of the street, as cars passed between them.

Darren was not bothered. It even amused him that this man was yelling aggressively while turning in the other direction. Darren was aware that he was staring at this man. Something about him drew his attention. Then it struck him. This was not the first time he had seen this man. The man was older, more worn-out, but still irrationally aggressive. He had formed Darren's first impressions of men. It was his father.

As he watched, familiar emotions stirred in him. Fear. He froze, then he had the impulse to run. This lasted a second. His instincts reminded him he was not a four-year-old boy scared of the large angry man threatening his mother. He was a grown soldier. His fists clenched and eyes widened. He edged forward, visualising himself running across the road and connecting his fist with his father's face. He savoured this vision. It was so satisfying to think of hurting him. After all he had done to Jane, the fear and misery he had inflicted.

His fist loosened. He breathed in deeply. His father was storming away and Darren calmed down. He wanted to be a better man; calm, disciplined and controlled. The opposite of his father: vile and reckless aggression, inflicting harm on everyone around him. He was a better man. He had a job, he earned money, he had looked after Jane and he did not hurt people. He pitied the man he had seen across the road. He took it as an example of what not to be. Darren walked away. He walked taller as he went.

As he arrived at his grandparents' home he was still calming down. His nerves were starting to settle and he was less agitated. He would not mention the sight of his father to either his grandparents or his mother.

He knocked on the door. His grandparents took longer and longer to open the door. This was on account of his grandparents' deteriorating health. It was Dawn who answered the door.

As the door opened and she looked up at Darren, her face made the same delighted expression it always made. A large smile broke across her wrinkled face and she beamed at Darren in her doorway.

'Oh, hello, Darren. I was hoping you would call in.'

He crossed the threshold and felt comfortable and happy. Entering the house, he left his problems at the door.

Dawn hobbled into the house ahead of him. Her stature was becoming more curved and she relied on a grey crutch. Despite her aged body, her hair remained brown.

Darren followed her into the kitchen and soon they were sitting at the table with a cup of tea each. Despite her health, Darren had received a stern word when he tried to help her make the drinks.

'It's a shame you weren't here earlier. Had you been here twenty minutes ago you would have seen Marley.'

Darren nodded. He had no idea who Marley was, but it was easier to nod along.

'She was asking after you of course. She had to leave early to pick up her prescription. Poor woman. My hip aches a bit but hers is just awful...'

Dawn carried on talking and Darren sat back half-listening. Her conversation moved from a deliberation of why Marley's hip would hurt so much, which Dawn imagined was the fault of the junior doctor being too young and not fitting the replacement in properly, to a brief reflection of how, in her day, doctors were always old, never a young doctor to be seen. You can't trust a young doctor. No experience, you wouldn't catch some young doctor practising on her like that. She wasn't a medical experiment. She then mentioned how she didn't trust dentists, young or old. People who spend their time prodding other people's teeth weren't the type to be trusted. Finally, she said:

'Your granddad should be back soon. He'll be glad to see you.'

Darren suddenly realised he was supposed to answer.

'Good,' he replied.

'He went out to buy a paper but he's been gone an hour. He's probably smoking. Says he's quit but thinks I can't smell it on him when he walks in,' said Dawn shaking her head.

Dawn was about to ask Darren about Jane and this man she had mentioned to them. She had been unsure whether to ask Darren directly. She was stopped by the sound of Frank walking through the door.

'Talk of the devil,' muttered Dawn as they heard Frank proceeding though the house. As he entered the kitchen Darren and Dawn could smell the smoke. Dawn passed Darren a knowing look.

'Hello, this is a nice surprise!' said Frank as he saw Darren.

Dawn rose like clockwork to make Frank a drink. Frank placed some biscuits and a newspaper on the table before sitting down opposite Darren.

'How are things going, Darren?'

'I'm all right, thanks.'

'Good. Army life OK?' He always asked this question with a slight hesitancy.

'Well...' replied Darren. 'Actually, now you're here, I have some news.'

'Oh, right.'

'It's not great, but I'm going on a tour of duty. Next month.'

'Oh... right.'

Darren could see Frank's demeanour change. His granddad had been so friendly and engaging up to this point. Now his arms folded around his large gut and his head dropped slightly but noticeably. He leaned back in his chair. He broke eye contact with Darren.

Darren had felt nervous before announcing this, and here was the reason. He knew that his granddad was not sympathetic to his career.

Dawn had stopped making the tea in the kitchen and came to stand in the room by Frank. She leaned on her crutch but did not speak. The atmosphere in the room reflected that of a courtroom. Darren felt like he had just been found guilty of a crime he was not even sure he had committed.

'I know it's not great news,' he said in defence. 'But I guess it's part of the job.'

'So... are you going to go?' asked Frank, still not looking at Darren.

'I guess so, yeah...'

'Where are you being sent?' Frank tried to sound normal but was struggling with the pretence.

'The Middle East.'

Darren was surprised his granddad didn't guess the answer. It was all over the news, the countries being attacked by terrorist groups and even the fall of cities. The last report he had seen was how desperate the defending forces were and how they had called to the West for more help.

Frank, still not looking at Darren, looked up at Dawn. She looked back at him. Darren could sense a non-verbal conversation going on between them. Darren interjected.

'I won't be on the front line or anything. The local forces have been drafted there, we're just supporting the rear, making sure it stays peaceful. It's like a pre-emptive prevention mission.'

The longer his grandparents stayed silent, the harder it was for Darren.

'I'll only be gone a few months.'

Dawn broke their silence first.

'It's all right, Darren. We just worry. We want you to be safe and your mum struggles, so we just hoped you would be around. Especially now she's mentioned a new man.'

Darren understood this. He wanted to be around as well, but it was his job. He had to go.

'They said it won't be dangerous or anything. Just patrolling a city, helping the security.'

Frank remained quiet, now looking out of the window. Dawn smiled at Darren. Not her usual, full, happy smile; it was a half-smile, forced, hinting at her disappointment.

She retreated into the kitchen. As she left, Frank turned around. He finally looked at Darren, who couldn't read his expression.

'I'm worried about your mum, Darren. She might struggle with you being away for so long.'

Darren thought bitterly about her new man. Perhaps *he* would make sure she was OK.

'The other problem I have, and I'm going to tell you because you should know. I don't think it's right. You need to think carefully about what you're doing.'

Dawn appeared in the room again. She had still not finished the tea she was making. She was looking at Frank. Her expression suggested she was mentally trying to tell him that this conversation was not necessary.

Darren frowned and Frank continued.

'I'm only an old man now and maybe I'm stuck in the past. I was always political, Darren. I've always been a socialist. Maybe I'm a dinosaur from the past, and maybe the world has moved on. But for what it's worth... I don't know what they've told you in the army... but the army going out there isn't going to make anyone safer. It's going to make things worse. It's going to make us less safe here at home.'

Darren didn't understand. It was obvious to him that where he was being sent there was a real threat, not just to the local people but also to this country. It was all over the news how vile this threat in the Middle East was. They needed to beat the terrorists, and had a duty to help.

'Right...' replied Darren, a puzzled look on his face.

'The way I see it, Darren, this country has been going over to other people's countries for hundreds of years. We went over there taking their stuff, exploiting their people and all that. I think it makes people angry. I think it has really messed things up.'

'We're not going there to take anything, though, we're going to help stop the terrorists. They're killing civilians, burning people alive...'

'I know that, Darren, I know they aren't good people. But they haven't come from nowhere. It's more complicated. Let me try and explain how I see it. If I lived over there, in one of these countries, and I saw all these foreign soldiers coming over all the time walking in my streets, and I knew that they had been coming over for years in the past and ruling our country. Then I saw that if our country wasn't trading or doing what America said, and then got invaded, I think I would get angry, Darren. Do you see what I mean?'

'Not really...'

'What I'm trying to say is that it might look like you're going over there to help, but you've got to look at why these terrorists started. It's like in Ireland. The IRA did some bad things, I know, but it's because they felt that they were always being controlled. They were fighting back against what they saw as an injustice. They weren't doing bad things for fun, they really felt they were fighting for something. When we sent soldiers over there it made things worse. These terrorists might be worse than the Irish, I don't know, but the more we go over there the more they're going to fight back. At some point, someone needs to start thinking about the bigger picture...'

'I don't understand,' said Darren. He could feel his heart pounding. He was quite angry. 'These people are attacking civilians in the Middle East and want to attack us. Someone needs to stop them, and we need to step up.'

Frank sighed and looked over at Darren. He wasn't going to drop this.

'I know, Darren, but why are they attacking civilians and why are they wanting to attack us? Islam is a peaceful religion, but they find the parts in their book that allow them to do bad things. Why is that?'

Darren was about to answer back. He could feel his stomach tensing and he was ready to shout at his granddad in exasperation. Why could he not understand that the terrorists needed to be stopped?

At this point Dawn said:

'Darren, listen, your granddad is just worried that you may not know about the bigger picture. It's complicated. We know you're doing it for the right reasons.'

'Yeah, I am,' replied Darren sharply.

'And I know that Frank knows that.' Frank looked out of the window again. 'So, you have to make your own mind up about what you do.'

Frank turned around suddenly. Dawn watched him closely.

'One last point now...'

'Frank, you've said what you need to say.'

'One last point, Dawn, just so I know I've said it.' Dawn gave way. 'Darren, I'm sorry I've spoken the way I have, but I just want you to know. What I'm really worried about is that you're putting yourself at risk for other people. I know they say it's about keeping us safe, but maybe there's other reasons, Darren. That's all. I'm just upset to think of my grandson being in danger for dishonourable reasons.'

Darren nodded, though he didn't know what his granddad meant. His feelings of anger subsided, replaced by an upset disappointment. This was the first time he had ever felt that his grandparents may feel negatively about him. He wanted to leave.

Dawn disappeared back to the kitchen and Frank sat quietly. Darren announced he had to leave. He called goodbye to Dawn and departed quickly. His grandparents said goodbye, but without the usual warmth; Darren left before they had a chance to speak.

He simply didn't want to stay there. They could say what they wanted to him; he had a duty to his friends and to the army. He understood that people would be concerned for him but what else could he do?

As he walked down the street past the terraced houses and back towards the centre of town, Darren dwelt on Frank's warnings. He was upset with the way his news had been received. He could not accept what his granddad had said. No matter what he did, the army would be deployed to the Middle East, and he was not going to let anyone down.

Frank's words continued to play on his mind. They fed the doubts that already lurked there about the impact of his leaving on Jane. He had to tell her today and he dreaded the thought. Having seen how Dawn and Frank reacted, he doubted his mother would be much more reasonable.

Darren didn't go straight back to Milltown. He delayed the journey in the hope that his mother's new man would have already gone home.

Chapter Fifteen

Darren was deployed. So was Abdul. Abdul's head now rested against the concrete wall of a first-floor flat. The room in which he sat was dark despite the sun shining on the world outside; shutters covered the small windows, allowing only the smallest light to trickle through. The darkened room was silent. It had the atmosphere of a tomb. Abdul could hear his heart beating in his chest. He could hear Adam lightly breathing next to him.

Adam sat contemplative, almost meditative. Over his crossed legs lay his gun, which he slowly fingered while lost in thought.

Abdul's own gun lay next to him. He felt uncomfortable holding it because of its size. Now and then he reached out to touch it, checking it was still there.

They shared the room with six other recruits. All dressed in black, all were still and all were silent. Hardly a whisper passed among them. Now and then one would rise and pace around the small room before returning to sit. Occasionally a noise would be heard in the corridor outside. The men in the flat would become tense until they knew that the disturbance was of no consequence to them.

The room itself felt like it was waiting.

Abdul trawled through his recent experiences. If that lonely boy who had fled Milltown now had someone to speak with, there would be so much he could share.

He could talk about the stress of travelling across Europe and the constant fear of being caught. He felt this fear like a weight around his neck. He would talk about the constant waiting, surrounded by comrades with whom he shared no common language. He could tell of being smuggled into Turkey, almost buckling under the weight of his fear. Then an even more uncomfortable journey before the illegal crossing into a sun-baked wilderness unlike anything he had ever known. He would be able to tell of a desperate journey across this unknown landscape in sweltering temperatures.

All the while reliant on strangers they did not know they could trust.

Aside from the travel, there was the experience. Placing trust in strangers; the hope that these strangers would be able to navigate borders and avoid security. There was the meeting with new people who showed little care or interest in either him or Adam. The food and the sleep he snatched on this journey were pitiable.

If Abdul had someone to speak with, he would explain arriving in a hidden training camp, detached from society. He could tell of learning to use a gun and exercising in excruciating heat. He could talk of failure, feeling like he was letting people down. He felt the embarrassment of appearing incapable in front of others who seemed so much more advanced than himself.

He witnessed darker things as well. Watching prisoners be tortured and scream through the pain. All the while, angry propaganda was a constant, reminding of the evils of the West.

Finally, buried deep in his mind, were lingering thoughts of his family. A guilt nested in his head, for the mother he had left, for the brother he had maimed and for the misery he had caused. As he felt like a failure in the camp, slowly he started to miss what he had left behind.

There was so much Abdul would be able to tell. For the first time, he had stories but no one to hear him.

Adam always supported him. When Abdul struggled with his fitness or was belittled by a leader, Adam was a pillar of strength. He had taken to their new life with an enthusiasm Abdul lacked. In the darkest moments of their journey, it had been Adam who maintained confidence and control. Adam remained convinced that this is where he should be. He had shown Abdul all the patience and love of a brother. Abdul was in awe of Adam.

Abdul had stayed and had coped, despite his growing doubts. In the UK he would now be labelled a terrorist and a traitor. These labels did not truly capture the position of

Abdul. He had left a life in the UK that felt hopeless, following a spiritual brother into what he believed would be a life of glory and heroism. He had arrived in another bleak and anonymous existence. Trained like a dog, fed enough to survive and drilled with propaganda, this life was no real improvement. He had been in a terrorist camp, but he didn't feel like one of them. While Adam stayed because he believed in the cause, Abdul stayed because there was no way out. Even if he could escape, where would he go or what would he do? Was there anywhere in the world for him?

He did still feel that the West was corrupt. Yet he did not see how him being in the Middle East was contributing to a better world. He did not air this concern; he would do nothing to upset or hurt Adam. He was not going to disappoint him now.

In the quiet dark room, these memories and doubts rolled through Abdul's mind. Surrounded by the other men, he waited. The longer they stayed, the harder it was to remember a time when their sole purpose had not been sitting and waiting. Hours had passed but, for all these men knew, it could have been weeks.

Neither Abdul nor Adam was aware of the full deliberations that had brought them to this room, in this block, in this town. They had only been passive objects moved at the orders of their leaders.

Prior to this town, they had been in a camp high in the hills, the fourth place they had stayed in however many months or years they had been away. The camp had a miserable atmosphere, leaving Abdul feeling on edge during their time there. While staying here, one of the superior leaders had taken them aside and informed them that, with some other recruits, they were to be smuggled into the town to take part in an operation.

And so it happened. One night, they had been handed their passports, hidden deep in a truck, surrounded by boxes and smuggled through the Western military checkpoints. There was neither discussion nor conversation. Without any prior experience of fighting, only the training they had received, they were moved like cattle and hidden in the town. They were placed in the flat.

Both young men were unaware of the decisions taken by leaders in darkened rooms in their mountain camps. The recruits were not privy to the malicious schemes, born of the desire to punish their enemies. Had Abdul heard the discussions of the leadership he would perhaps have understood his role better; he was little more than a pawn.

While Abdul had been in the camp, intelligence had been received by the leaders that the British army were patrolling local cities while native security forces were transferred to the front. While not engaging the enemy, they were making their presence known. The intelligence told of regular patrols of small groups of soldiers in the local towns. On the dusty streets in daylight, they seemed easy targets.

Given the opportunity to attack Western soldiers directly, the leadership had considered an operation. While they knew that a direct attack may lead to repercussions, the morale of their own troops would only rise knowing they could directly strike their true enemies. They would spread fear directly to their enemies, letting them know they were not beyond their reach.

Plans were developed, the town for the strike was selected. Locals were co-opted and weapons were smuggled in. Then came the decision of who to send. The best recruits were chosen, those who had experience of fighting or those who had excelled in training; those who truly deserved the honour of attacking Western soldiers. It was in this discussion that Adam and Abdul's fate was decided. A smiling and scarred former fighter member of the highest leadership in a quiet voice had said: 'We have two British recruits in the camp, we should send them also. The British should know their society is breeding soldiers of Islam.'

The propaganda gains of British terrorists attacking British soldiers made the leadership water at the mouth. Some almost giggled like children thinking of the British seeing their own citizens recruited as terrorists. They were added to the group; their passports returned so that in the event of their deaths, they would be identified with ease.

Thus, Adam and Abdul now waited in the darkened room with the hardened recruits around them. Both felt nervous, yet this was mitigated by a fatalism. They were here and what would happen would happen.

*

While Abdul sat waiting for his fate, Darren set out on patrol. He had spent two months in the Middle East now, and relished the thought of returning home soon. His day-to-day existence in this land had been nothing but mundane. His life had rotated between staying in the barracks and going on patrol. There were daily duties which he carried out in between long periods of waiting.

Though he wanted to return, he felt uneasy about this; his mother's new man and his grandfather's disappointment made him apprehensive about seeing his family again. Despite this, he still wanted to be away from the exhausting boredom of his current existence.

The land and climate had struck Darren in much the same way that it had Abdul. The two young men, having known nothing other than the drab English winters and occasionally sunny summers, were awed by the exhausting heat. The hot air and dry earth stood in stark contrast to the damp and grey of Milltown.

Today, two months into his stay, Darren walked in the hot streets of the local town. The heat made him sweat under the weight of his equipment. His gun felt heavy and his boots were uncomfortable. As the patrol passed in the shade of buildings, Darren enjoyed the slightly cooler air.

The patrol consisted of four soldiers. Previous patrols had larger numbers; however, as there had been no intelligence of threats to the patrols, command had decided to reduce their size and send the troops out more frequently.

As they walked through the streets, the local people hardly noticed them. They were so used to seeing the soldiers lumbering through their town that they seemed part of the scenery. Yet an outsider, arriving here for the first time, would certainly notice the soldiers looking out of place. From their Western culture, the soldiers bearing their technologically advanced and expensive equipment differed from the local people. The local cars were old, the people's clothes were generally worn-looking; they appeared slightly malnourished. The soldiers, in their physical condition, looked far removed from any experience of hunger. There was no active fighting in the town but the impact of war was evident.

The patrols among these tired-looking people in this dry town had rarely led to any excitement. In one instance, Darren had broken up a fight between two men over an accusation of theft. Another time local children had pelted the soldiers with stones. In all, however, had you asked one of these soldiers to record their memoirs of this tour, they would hardly have filled a page.

From the barracks in England to this sweltering land, Darren had grown closer to his comrades. The daily banter among them had formed a feeling of community. All were foreign on this soil and plagued by the same boredom.

The course of their patrol today led them onto the quieter backstreets. The roads were narrower and fewer pedestrians were wandering. Turning away from the main streets, they felt the vibrancy of the city dissipating as they entered quieter residential areas.

The four soldiers turned into another street. A number of parked cars lined the street, in front of medium sized concrete apartments. The blocks were built close together and the area felt cramped. They cast their shadow onto the street.

As they stepped onto this street Darren dropped to the back of the group. He looked all around as they paced forward.

He slowed down. Seven or eight civilians also walked in this place, none bothering with the soldiers, except one.

Out ahead of them this civilian, holding a phone to his ear, kept looking up at the soldiers. He was stationary and kept looking up at the patrol. He didn't seem relaxed. Darren kept watching him.

Something was not right. The soldier at the head of the patrol passed a parked car. Darren called out.

As Darren called, the man on the phone ran. The soldiers looked alert. This was not right. Darren stepped forward.

*

Then the explosion. A car bomb detonated near to where the man had been standing. The soldier at the front of the group blasted forward, debilitated. The remaining soldiers, in shock, gathered themselves as the blast resonated.

Dust covered the street and people screamed.

Then gunfire. Bullets penetrated the chaotic scene.

Abdul, holding his gun, rushed from the flat with his comrades and down into the street. His heart pounded; he was short of breath. Adam touched his shoulder. A small comforting relief. Adam readied his gun.

From the doorway, following the comrades, Adam presented himself to the enemy. A volley of fire met them.

Abdul waited. He shook. The gunfire was relentless.

There was no way out. He took a deep breath and left the safety of the doorway, into the gunfire.

Looking into the chaos, he saw his comrades starting to run. They disappeared into the city. Through the dust, he saw a body lying lifeless in the street. He dropped his gun. The chaos faded. He only saw the body.

The body lay like his brother's had. Blood seeped from the body and into the dusty street. Kneeling next to the body, blood soaked into his black garments.

Abdul knelt over the corpse of Adam. The life drained fast from his body. Fear gave way to grief. An overwhelming grief. It reduced the fear of death to a nothingness.

*

The street was empty now. The enemy had fled from the chaos, leaving stillness and silence. Darren's three comrades lay dead, accompanied by four of their enemies.

Darren emerged from the safety of his cover. He saw the corpses, two of which he had killed. He caught his breath. His first emotion was loneliness. The only soldier left from his patrol.

Darren was reaching for his radio when he noticed Abdul. Kneeling in the centre of the street, Abdul clutched the corpse of Adam. Grief-stricken, he didn't even look up. He was fixated on his fallen friend.

Bloody-minded, Darren dropped the radio. He stepped towards him. He planned to kill him. He savoured the thought of killing him.

He pulled out his hand-gun. This would be an intimate kill. He wanted to look this boy in the eye as he blasted the life from him.

Darren registered the danger. He knew he shouldn't leave himself exposed to another attack. He also knew that if anyone witnessed this kill, there may be a court martial. He continued approaching, driven by deathly impulses.

Abdul looked up. Tears rolled down his cheeks, his mouth hung open. His grief-stricken face looked towards the approaching soldier; the mask he had worn hung limply around his neck. A hand covered in the blood of Adam rose to move tears from his cheek. Moving the tear, he wiped blood across his face.

The soldier approached, but Abdul did not move. Hopelessness filled him; he knew there was no escape. The soldier was too close. He would not even be on his feet before being shot down like a dog.

Dark thoughts surfaced. Frozen, he knew that death was his only escape. Perhaps death was what he wanted. Perhaps death was the plan God had for him and Adam.

Darren looked into the face of his enemy. He wanted to see him before he pulled the trigger. He looked into the red eyes of the boy that stared intently back at the killer.

Looking at these eyes, Darren was taken back. Moments from his past surged to the forefront of his mind. He had seen eyes like this before, upset, pleading and innocent. Visions of his earliest memories, of his mother, flew through his mind, her fear of his father wielding his power. Memories of victims at school and their misery echoed in his memory. Lurking in his mind was a memory that told him he had seen *these* eyes before. Unable to place them, he only remembered the emotion they aroused in him; the pity and sadness he felt. The guilt of seeing a broken creature at the mercy of the world around him. For a moment, he was outside his flat in Milltown; he had seen this powerless body before.

The impulses for murder disappeared. Darren's grip on the trigger eroded. Feelings of guilt and shame subsumed him as he looked on the grief-stricken wreck before him. A memory of his grandfather entered his mind.

The gun lowered. 'Go,' he said to Abdul.

Abdul did not move. Perplexed, he stayed with Adam. He could not move.

'Go!' ordered the soldier again.

He accompanied his order with a shot. The bullet landed close to Abdul.

Now, finally, instinct took hold of Abdul. He stumbled backwards, scrambling to his feet. He fled into the empty streets, lost. He didn't know where he would go, or why he was running.

He fled from the soldier who had been intent on his murder. This soldier stood alone, looking at the ruined world around him. He stood in the street with debris and death. A nameless emotion filled his body; he was unable to even begin to articulate these thoughts. A loaded gun remained in his hand.

*

The next day the UK national press would report the assault on the British soldiers. Hard-line papers would report on the brutal ambush, highlighting the barbarity of the enemy. They would question whether the local population even deserved

UK soldiers to be patrolling their streets. They would ask who the perpetrators were and if they could be found.

There would be unanimous outrage that one of the dead attackers was found with a British passport in their belongings. Adam's name would swamp the press; some would call for the citizenship of traitors to be revoked.

The more thoughtful papers would question what British soldiers were doing in the streets and why there had not been intelligence about these attacks. They would question army practices and what precautions should have been taken to avoid these deaths.

There would be omissions in the reporting as well. None would question the ethics behind whether UK soldiers should be there in the first place. There was an underlying assumption that it was acceptable for the UK to place boots on the ground in another country. None reflected on the outrage that would occur should another nation deploy troops in the UK to help those, for instance, starving on our streets.

The most glaring omission from the papers was also the most telling.

Buried deep in the intelligence reports confirming the deaths of four British soldiers, a crucial fact was censored, even from their families. The final soldier, Darren Blackwater, on his first tour of duty, died with a bullet in his head. Not fired by an enemy soldier in a second ambush, this bullet was British made. The bullet that blasted out his brains was fired by his own gun, his own finger pulling the trigger.

This bullet was the only way to cleanse the chaos that polluted his mind.

Other recent titles from Armley Press

Before the Gulf
John Lake
'A great read on so many levels'

The Heat of the Summer
Liam Randles
'A truly engrossing novel'

Dying is the Last Thing You Ever Want to Do
Michael Yates
'Gripping, intelligent, authentic and… tremendous fun!'

Whoosh!
Ray Brown
'I laughed out loud… then laughed out loud again'

The Last Sane Man on Earth
Nathan O'Hagan
'A satirical, poignant and hilarious modern classic'

Sex & Death and other stories
Ivor Tymchak
'Surprising, disturbing and funny'

Thurso
P. James Callahan
'Unflinching and raw… a "make you think" dark debut'

www.ingramcontent.com/pod-product-compliance
Ingram Content Group UK Ltd.
Pitfield, Milton Keynes, MK11 3LW, UK
UKHW042016190726
13854UKWH00005B/2312